RECKLESS

Written and illustrated by

CORNELIA
FUNKE

❧ A story found and told by ❧
Cornelia Funke and Lionel Wigram

Translated by Oliver Latsch

Little, Brown and Company
New York Boston

Little, Brown and Company

Hachette Book Group
237 Park Avenue, New York, NY 10017
Visit our website at www.lb-teens.com

Little, Brown and Company is a division of Hachette Book Group, Inc.
The Little, Brown name and logo are trademarks of Hachette Book Group, Inc.

First Paperback Edition: September 2011
First published in hardcover in September 2010 by Little, Brown and Company

The characters and events portrayed in this book are fictitious. Any similarity to real persons,
living or dead, is coincidental and not intended by the author.

Library of Congress Cataloging-in-Publication Data

Funke, Cornelia.
    Reckless / Cornelia Funke ; translated by Oliver Latsch. — 1st ed.
        p. cm.
    Summary: Jacob and Will Reckless have looked out for each other ever since their father
disappeared, but when Jacob discovers a magical mirror that transports him to a warring
world populated by witches, fairies, and dwarfs, he keeps it to himself until Will follows him
one day, with dire consequences.
    ISBN 978-0-316-05609-0 (hc) / ISBN 978-0-316-05607-6 (pb)
    [1. Fantasy. 2. Brothers—Fiction. 3. Adventure and adventurers—Fiction. 4. Magic—
Fiction.] I. Latsch, Oliver. II. Title.
    PZ7.F96624Re 2010
    [Fic]—dc22   2010006877

10 9 8 7 6 5 4 3 2 1

RRD-C

Book design by Alison Impey

Printed in the United States of America

FOR LIONEL, who found the door to this story and who so often knew more about it than I did, friend and finder of ideas, indispensable on either side of the mirror.

AND FOR OLIVER, who again and again tailored English clothes for this story so that the Englishman and the German could tell it together.

1. ONCE UPON A TIME

The night breathed through the apartment like a dark animal. The ticking of a clock. The groan of a floorboard as he slipped out of his room. All was drowned by its silence. But Jacob loved the night. He felt it on his skin like a promise. Like a cloak woven from freedom and danger.

Outside the stars were paled by the glaring lights of the city, and the large apartment was

stale with his mother's sorrow. She did not wake as Jacob stole into her room, even when he carefully opened the drawer of her nightstand. The key lay right next to the pills that let her sleep. Its cool metal nestled in his hand as he stepped back out into the dark corridor.

There was still a light burning in his brother's room—Will was afraid of the dark—and Jacob made sure he was fast asleep before unlocking the door to their father's study. Their mother had not entered there since his disappearance, but for Jacob this was not the first time he had snuck into the empty room to search for the answers she did not want to give.

It still looked as if John Reckless had last sat in his desk chair less than an hour ago, instead of more than a year. The sweater he had worn so often hung over the chair, and a used tea bag was desiccating on a plate next to his calendar, which still showed the weeks of a passed year.

Come back! Jacob wrote it with his finger on the fogged-up window, on the dusty desk, and on the glass panels of the cabinet that still held the old pistols his father had collected. But the room remained silent—and empty. He was twelve and no longer had a father. Jacob kicked at the drawers he had searched in vain for so many nights. In a silent rage, he yanked the books and magazines from the shelves, tore down the model airplanes that hung above the desk, ashamed at how proud he had once been when his father had allowed him to paint one with red varnish.

Come back! He wanted to scream it through the streets that cut their gleaming paths through the city blocks seven stories below, scream it at the thousand windows that punched squares of light into the night.

The sheet of paper slipped out of a book on airplane propulsion. Jacob only picked it up because he thought he recognized his father's handwriting on it, though he quickly realized his error. Symbols and equations, a sketch of a peacock, a sun, two moons. None of it made any sense. Except for the one sentence he spotted on the reverse side:

THE MIRROR WILL OPEN ONLY FOR HE WHO CANNOT SEE HIMSELF.

Jacob turned around—and his glance was met by his own reflection.

The mirror. He still remembered very well the day his father had mounted it on the wall. It hung between the shelves like a shimmering eye, a glassy abyss that cast back a warped reflection of everything John Reckless had left behind: his desk, the old pistols, his books—and his elder son.

The glass was so uneven one could barely recognize one's own reflection, and it was darker than other mirrors, but the rose tendrils winding across the silver frame looked so real they seemed ready to wilt at any moment.

THE MIRROR WILL OPEN ONLY FOR HE WHO CANNOT SEE HIMSELF.

Jacob closed his eyes.

He turned back to the mirror.

Felt behind the frame for some kind of lock or latch.

Nothing.

Only his reflection was looking him straight in the eye.

It took quite a while before Jacob understood.

His hand was barely large enough to cover the distorted reflection of his face. But the cool glass clung to his fingers as if it had been waiting for them, and suddenly the room he saw in the mirror was no longer his father's study.

Jacob turned around.

Moonlight fell through two narrow windows onto gray walls, and his naked feet stood on wooden floorboards covered with acorn shells and the gnawed bones of birds. The room was bigger than his father's study, and above him cobwebs hung like veils from the rafters of a roof.

Where was he? He stepped toward one of the windows, the moonlight painting patterns on his skin. The bloody feathers of a bird stuck to the rough ledge, and far below he saw scorched walls and black hills with a few lost lights glimmering in the distance. He was in a tower. Gone were the sea of houses, the bright streets—everything he knew was gone. And high among the stars were two moons, the smaller one as red as a rusty coin.

Jacob looked back at the mirror, and in it he saw the fear on his face. But fear was an emotion he had grown to like. It lured him to dark places, through forbidden doors, and away from himself, and even the yearning for his father could be drowned in it.

There was no door in the gray walls, just a trapdoor in the floor. When Jacob opened it, he saw the remains of a burnt staircase melting into the darkness below, and for a moment he thought he spotted a tiny figure climbing up the stones. But a sudden rasp made him wheel around.

Cobwebs fell down on him as something jumped onto his neck with a hoarse growl. It sounded like an animal, but the contorted face flashing its teeth at his throat looked as pale and wrinkled as an old man's. It was much smaller than Jacob, and as spindly as an insect. Its clothes seemed to be made of cobwebs, its white hair hung down to its hips, and when Jacob grabbed for its thin neck, the creature sank its yellow teeth deep into his hand. Screaming, he punched the attacker off his shoulder and stumbled toward the mirror. The spidery creature got to its feet again, licking his blood from its lips, but before it could reach him Jacob was already pressing his hand on the reflection of his scared face. Immediately, the scrawny figure disappeared, together with the gray walls, and behind him Jacob could once again see his father's desk.

"Jacob?"

His brother's voice barely registered over the beating of his heart. Jacob gasped for air and backed away from the mirror.

"Jake? Are you in there?"

He pulled his sleeve over his mauled hand and quietly opened the door.

Will's eyes were wide with fear. He'd had another bad dream. Little brother. Will always followed him like a puppy, and Jacob protected him in the schoolyard and in the park. Sometimes he even managed to forgive Will that their mother loved him more.

"Mom says we shouldn't go in there."

"Since when do I do what Mom says? If you tell on me, I won't take you to the park ever again."

Jacob thought he could feel the glass of the mirror like ice on the back of his neck. Will peered past him, but he quickly lowered his head as Jacob pulled the door shut behind them. Will. Careful where Jacob was rash, tender where he was short-tempered, and calm where he was restless. Jacob took his hand. Will noticed the blood on his fingers and gave him a quizzical look, but Jacob just quietly pushed him into his room.

What the mirror had shown him was his. His alone.

2. TWELVE YEARS LATER

The sun already stood low over the burnt walls of the ruin, but Will was still asleep, exhausted from the pain that had been shaking him for days.

One mistake, Jacob, after all those years of caution.

He got up and covered Will with his coat.

All the years in which Jacob had a whole world

to himself. All the years during which that strange world had become home. By the time Jacob was fifteen, he had already snuck behind the mirror for weeks at a time. When he was sixteen, he no longer even counted the months, and still he had kept his secret. Until the one time when he had been in too much of a rush. *Stop it, Jacob! It can't be changed.*

The wounds on his brother's throat had healed well, but the stone was already showing on his left forearm. The pale green veins were spreading toward his hand, shimmering in Will's skin like polished marble.

Just one mistake.

Jacob leaned against one of the sooty columns and looked up toward the tower that housed the mirror. He had never gone through it without first making sure Will and his mother were asleep. But since she had died there had just been one more empty room on the other side, and he had been keen to press his hand against the dark glass again and get away. Far away.

Impatience, Jacob. Say it as it is. After all, it's one of your most prominent character traits.

He could still see Will's face appear behind him in the mirror, distorted by the dark glass. *"Where are you going, Jacob?"* A late flight to Boston, a trip to Europe; there had been so many excuses over the years. Jacob was just as creative a liar as his father had been. But this time his hand had already pressed against the cool glass—and Will had, of course, followed his example.

Little brother.

"He already smells like them." Fox appeared out of the shadows cast by the crumbled walls. Her fur was as red as if autumn itself had lent her its colors, except where the trap had streaked the hind leg with pale scars. It had been five years since Jacob had freed her, and the vixen had not left his side since. She guarded his sleep, warned him of dangers that his dull human senses could not detect, and she gave advice that was best followed.

One mistake.

Jacob stepped through the arched doorway in which the scorched remnants of the castle's main door were still hanging on the warped hinges. On the steps in front, a Heinzel was collecting acorns from the cracked stones. He quickly scampered off as Jacob's shadow fell on him. Red eyes above a pointy nose, pants and shirt sewn from stolen human clothes. The ruin was swarming with them.

"Send him back! That's what we came here for, isn't it?" The impatience in Fox's voice was hard to miss.

But Jacob shook his head. "Bringing him here was

a mistake. There's nothing on the other side that can help him."

Jacob had told Fox about the world he came from, but she never really wanted to hear about it. What she knew was enough: that it was the place to which he disappeared far too often, only to bring back memories that followed him like shadows.

"And? What do you think will happen to him here?"

Fox did not say it, but Jacob knew what she was thinking. In her world, fathers killed their own sons as soon as they discovered the stone in their skin.

He looked down toward the foot of the castle hill, where the red roofs were fading into the twilight. The first lights were coming on in Schwanstein. From a distance, the town looked like one of the pictures printed on gingerbread tins, but over the past years, railway tracks had begun to cut through the hills beyond, and gray smoke rose from the smokestacks of factories into the evening sky. The world behind the mirror wanted to grow up. However, the petrified flesh growing in his brother had not been sown by mechanical looms or any of the other modern achievements but by the old magic that still dwelled in its hills and forests.

A Gold-Raven landed next to Will on the cracked

tiles. Jacob shooed it away before it could croak one of its sinister spells into his brother's ear.

Will groaned in his sleep. The human skin did not yield to the stone without a fight. Jacob felt the pain as his own. Only his love for his brother had made him return to the other world, even though he'd done so less and less frequently over the years. His mother had threatened him with social services, she had cried, but she had never suspected where he vanished to. Will, however, had always wrapped his arms around Jacob, eagerly asking what he had brought for him. The shoes of a Heinzel, the cap of a Thumbling, a button made of elven glass, a piece of scaly Waterman skin—Will had hoarded Jacob's gifts under his mattress, and soon he began to regard the stories Jacob told him as fairy tales his brother invented only for him.

Now he knew how true they had all been.

Jacob pulled the coat over his brother's disfigured arm. The two moons were already in the sky.

"Keep an eye on him, Fox." He rose to his feet. "I'll be back soon."

"And where are you going? Jacob!" The vixen jumped into his path. "Nobody can help him."

"We'll see." He pushed her aside. "Don't let Will climb into the tower."

She looked after him as he walked down the steps. The only footprints on the mossy steps were his own. No human ventured up here. The ruin was thought to be cursed, and Jacob had heard dozens of stories about its demise, but after all these years he still didn't know who had left the mirror in its tower, just as he had never found out where his father had vanished to.

A Thumbling jumped at his collar. Jacob managed to grab him before he could steal the medallion he was wearing around his neck. On any other day, Jacob would have followed the little thief at once. Thumblings could hoard considerable treasures in the hollow trees where they built their nests. But he had already lost too much time.

One mistake, Jacob.

He would make it right again. But Fox's words followed him as he climbed down the steep hill.

Nobody can help him.

If she was right, soon he would no longer have a brother. Neither in this world nor in the other.

One mistake.

3. GOYL

The field over which Hentzau and his soldiers were riding still reeked of blood. The rain had filled the trenches with a muddy sludge. Behind the walls both sides had built for their protection lay abandoned rifles and bullet-riddled helmets. Kami'en had the horse cadavers and the human corpses burnt before they began to rot, but the dead Goyl still lay where they had fallen.

In just a few days, they would be all but indistinguishable from the rocks that protruded from the trampled earth, and the heads of those who had fought valiantly had already been sent to the main fortress, as was Goyl custom.

Another battle. Hentzau was tired of them, but he hoped that this would be the last one for a while. The Empress was finally ready to negotiate, and even Kami'en wanted peace. Hentzau covered his mouth as the wind blew the ash down from the hill where they had burnt the corpses. Six years aboveground, six years without the shelter of the rock between him and the sun. His eyes ached from all the light, and the air was again growing colder with every day, making his skin as brittle as chalk. Hentzau's skin resembled brown jasper—not the finest color for a Goyl. Hentzau was the first jasper Goyl to have risen to the highest military ranks. But then again, before Kami'en the Goyl had never had a King, and Hentzau liked his skin. Jasper provided much better camouflage than onyx or moonstone.

Kami'en had set up camp not far from the battlefield, in the hunting lodge of an imperial general who, together with most of his officers, had died in the battle.

The sentries guarding the destroyed gate saluted as Hentzau rode past them. The King's bloodhound. That's what they called him. His jasper shadow. Hentzau had served under Kami'en since they had first challenged the other chiefs. It had taken two years for them to kill them all, and for the Goyl to get their first King.

The drive leading up to the lodge was lined with statues, and not for the first time did Hentzau note with amusement how humans immortalized their gods and heroes with stone effigies while loathing his kind for their skin. Even the Doughskins had to admit it: Stone was the only thing that lasted.

The windows of the lodge had been bricked up, just as in all the buildings the Goyl had occupied, but only when he descended the steps to the cellars did Hentzau finally feel the soothing darkness that could be found belowground. Just a few gas lamps lit the vaults that now housed, instead of supplies and dusty trophies, the general staff of the King of the Goyl.

Kami'en. In their language, it meant nothing more than "stone." His father had governed one of the lower cities, but fathers did not count among the Goyl. It was the mothers who raised them, and by the age of nine Goyl were considered grown up and had to fend for themselves. At that age, most of them went to explore the Lower World, searching for undiscovered caves until the heat became too much even for their stone skins. Kami'en, however, had been interested only in the world above. For a long time, he had lived in one of the cave cities that had been built aboveground after the lower cities had become too crowded. There, he had survived two attacks by the humans, and that's when he began to study their weapons and their tactics, snuck into their towns and military camps. He was nineteen when he conquered his first human city.

The guards waved Hentzau in. Kami'en was standing in front of a map showing his conquests and the positions of his enemies. The figurines representing their troops had been made to his specifications after he'd won his first battle. The Goyl were carved from carnelian, the imperials were cast in silver, Lotharaine wore gold, the eastern lords donned copper, and Albion's troops marched in ivory. Soldiers, gunners, snipers, riders for the cavalry. Kami'en scrutinized them as if he were searching for a way to beat them all at once. He was wearing black, as he always did when he was out of uniform, and more than ever his pale red skin seemed to be made of fire. Never before had carnelian been the color of a leader. Onyx was the color of the Goyl elite.

Kami'en's mistress was wearing green, as usual, layers of emerald velvet that enveloped her like the petals of a flower. Even the most beautiful Goyl woman would have paled next to her, like a pebble next to polished moonstone, but Hentzau always impressed upon his soldiers not to look at her for too long. Her beauty was like a spider's venom, and not for nothing were there many stories of Fairies who, with a single glance, had turned men into thistles or helplessly wriggling fish. She and her sisters had been born of water, and Hentzau feared them as much as he feared the seas that gnawed at the rocks of his world.

The Fairy gave him a cursory glance as he entered. The Dark Fairy. The darkest of them all. Even her own sisters had cast her out. Many believed that she could read minds, but Hentzau didn't think so. She would have long killed him for what he thought about her.

He turned his back on her and bowed his head to his King. "You summoned me."

Kami'en took one of the silver figurines and weighed it in his hand. "I need you to find someone for me. A human who is growing petrified flesh."

Hentzau cast a quick glance at the Fairy.

"Where should I start?" he replied. "There are already thousands of them."

Man-Goyl. In the past, Hentzau had used his claws for killing, but now the spell of the Fairy let them sow petrified flesh. Like all Fairies, she could not bear children, so she gave Kami'en sons by letting every strike of his soldiers' claws turn one of his human enemies into Goyl. Nobody fought with less mercy than a Man-Goyl fighting against his former race, but Hentzau despised them just as much as he despised the Fairy who had created them with her sorcery.

A smile had snuck onto Kami'en's lips. No. The Fairy could not read Hentzau's thoughts, but his King could.

"Don't worry. The one I want you to find can be easily distinguished from the others." Kami'en placed the silver figurine back on the map. "The skin he is growing is jade."

The guards exchanged a quick look. Hentzau, however, just sneered. Lava-Men who boiled the blood of the earth, the eyeless bird that saw all, and the Goyl with the jade skin who gave invincibility to the King he served...stories told to children to fill the darkness underground.

"And which scout told you that?" Hentzau rubbed his aching skin. Soon the cold would have given it more cracks than fractured glass. "Have him executed. The Jade Goyl is a myth. Since when do you confuse myths with reality?"

The guards nervously ducked their heads. Any other Goyl would have paid for that remark with his life. Kami'en, however, just shrugged.

"Find him!" he said. "She dreamed of him."

She. The Fairy smoothed the velvet of her dress. Six fingers on each hand. Each one for a different curse. Hentzau felt the rage rise in him. It was the rage they all bore in their stony flesh, like the heat in the depths of the earth. He would die for his King if necessary, but to have to search for the daydreams of his mistress was something else.

"You need no Jade Goyl to make yourself invincible!"

Kami'en eyed him like a stranger.

Your Majesty. Hentzau now often caught himself not wanting to call him by his name.

"Find him," Kami'en repeated. "She says it's important, and so far she's always been right."

The Fairy stepped to his side. Hentzau pictured himself squeezing her pale neck. But not even that gave him comfort. She was immortal, and one day she would watch him die. Him and the King. And Kami'en's children and his children's children. They all were nothing but her mortal stone toys. But the King loved her. More than his two Goyl wives, who had given him three daughters and a son.

Because she has hexed him! Hentzau heard a whisper inside him. But he bowed his head and pressed his fist over his heart. "Whatever you command!"

"I saw him in the black forest." Even her voice sounded like water.

"That's more than sixty square miles!"

The Fairy smiled. Hentzau felt rage and fear choking his heart.

Without another word, she undid the pearl clasp with which she pinned her hair like a human woman, and brushed her hand through it. Black moths fluttered out from between her fingers; the pale spots on their wings looked like skulls. The guards quickly opened the doors as the insects swarmed toward them, and even Hentzau's soldiers, who had been waiting outside in the dark corridor, recoiled as the moths flew past. They all knew that their sting penetrated even Goyl skin.

The Fairy put the clasp back in her hair.

"Once they find him," she said, without looking at Hentzau, "they will come to you. And you will bring him to me. Immediately."

His men were staring at her through the open door, but they quickly lowered their heads as Hentzau turned around.

Fairy.

Damn her and the night she had suddenly appeared among their tents. The third battle, and their third victory. She had walked toward the King's tent as if the groans of their wounded and the white moon above their dead had summoned her. Hentzau had stepped into her path, but she had just walked through him, like liquid through porous stone, as if he, too, were already among the dead, and she had stolen his King's heart to fill her own heartless bosom with it.

Even Hentzau had to admit that the best weapons combined did not spread as much fear as her curse, which turned the flesh of their enemies into stone. Yet he was certain they would have still won the war without her, and that victory would have tasted so much sweeter.

"I will find the Jade Goyl without your moths," he said. "If he really is more than just a dream."

She answered him with a smile, which followed him back into the daylight that clouded his eyes and cracked his skin.

Damn her.

4. On the Other Side

Will's voice had sounded so different, Clara had barely recognized it. Nothing for weeks, and then this stranger on the phone who wouldn't really say why he had called.

The streets seemed even more congested than usual, and the trip was endless, until she finally stood in front of the old apartment building where he and his brother had grown up. Stone

faces stared down from the gray facade, their contorted features eroded by exhaust fumes. Clara couldn't help but look up at them as the doorman held the door for her. She was still wearing the pale green surgical gown under her coat. She had not taken the time to change. She had just run out of the hospital.

Will.

He had sounded so lost. Like someone who was drowning. Or someone who was saying farewell.

Clara pulled the grilled doors of the elevator shut behind her. She'd worn the same gown the first time she'd met Will, in front of the room where his mother had lain. Clara often worked weekends at the hospital, not only because she needed the money. Textbooks and universities made you forget all too easily that flesh and blood were actually very real.

Seventh floor.

The copper nameplate next to the door was so tarnished that Clara involuntarily wiped it with her sleeve.

RECKLESS. Will had often made fun of how that name did not suit him at all.

Unopened mail was piled up behind the door, but there was light in the hall.

"Will?"

She opened the door to his room.

Nothing.

He wasn't in the kitchen, either.

The apartment looked as if he hadn't been there in weeks. But Will had told her he was calling from here. Where was he?

Clara walked past his mother's empty room, and that of his brother, whom she had never met. *"Jacob is traveling."* Jacob was always traveling. Sometimes she wasn't sure whether he actually existed.

She stopped.

The door to his father's study was open. Will never entered that room. He ignored anything that had to do with his father.

Clara entered hesitantly. Bookshelves, a glass cabinet, a desk. The model planes above it wore dust on their wings, like dirty snow. The whole room was dusty, and so cold that she could see her breath.

A mirror hung between the shelves.

Clara stepped in front of it and let her fingers run over the silver roses that covered the frame. She had never seen anything so beautiful. The glass they surrounded was dark, as if the night had spilled onto it. It was misted up, and right where she saw the reflection of her face was the imprint of a hand.

5. SCHWANSTEIN

The light of the lanterns filled Schwanstein's streets like spilled milk. Gaslight, wooden wheels bumping over cobblestones, women in long skirts, their hems soaked from the rain. The damp autumn air smelled of smoke, and soot blackened the laundry that hung between the pointy gables. There was a railway station right opposite the old coach station, a telegraph

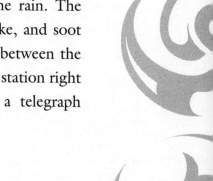

office, and a photographer who fixed stiff hats and ruffled skirts onto silver plates. Bicycles leaned against walls on which posters warned of Gold-Ravens and Watermen. Nowhere did the Mirrorworld emulate the other side as eagerly as in Schwanstein, and Jacob, of course, asked himself many times how much of it all had come through the mirror that hung in his father's study. The town's museum had many items on display that looked suspiciously like objects from the other world. A compass and a camera seemed so familiar to Jacob that he thought he recognized them as his father's, though nobody had been able to tell him where the stranger who had left them behind had vanished to.

The bells of the town were ringing in the evening as Jacob walked down the street that led to the market square. A Dwarf woman was selling roasted chestnuts in front of a bakery. Their sweet aroma mixed with the smell of the horse manure that was scattered all over the cobblestones. The idea of the combustion engine had not yet made it through the mirror, and the monument on the square showed a King on horseback who had hunted Giants in the surrounding hills. He was an ancestor of the reigning Empress, Therese of Austry, whose family had hunted not only

Giants but also Dragons so successfully that they were considered extinct within her realm. The paperboy who was standing next to the statue, shouting the news into the gathering dusk, had definitely never seen more than the footprint of a Giant or the scorch marks of Dragon fire on the town walls.

DECISIVE BATTLE. TERRIBLE LOSSES. GENERAL AMONG THE FALLEN. SECRET NEGOTIATIONS.

This world was at war, and it was not being won by humans. Four days had passed since he and Will had run into one of their patrols, but Jacob could still see them come out of the forest: three soldiers and an officer, their stone faces wet from the rain. Golden eyes. Black claws that tore into his brother's throat... Goyl.

"Look after your brother, Jacob."

He put three copper coins into the boy's grubby hand. The Heinzel sitting on the boy's shoulder eyed them suspiciously. Many Heinzel chose human companions who fed and clothed them—though that did little to improve their crabby dispositions.

"How far are the Goyl?" Jacob took a newspaper.

"Less than five miles from here." The boy pointed southeast. "With the wind right, we could hear their cannons. But it's been quiet since yesterday." He sounded almost disappointed. At his age, even war sounded like an adventure.

The imperial soldiers filing out of the tavern next to the church probably knew better. THE OGRE. Jacob had been witness to the events that had given the tavern its name and had cost its owner his right arm. Albert Chanute was standing behind the counter, wearing a grim expression, as Jacob entered the dingy taproom. Chanute was such a gross hulk of a man that people said he had Troll blood running through his veins, not a compliment in the Mirrorworld. But until the Ogre had chopped off his arm, Albert Chanute had been the best treasure hunter in all of Austry, and for many years Jacob had been his apprentice. Chanute had shown him everything he had needed to gather fame and fortune behind the mirror, and it had been Jacob who had prevented the Ogre from also hacking off Chanute's head.

Mementos of his glory days covered the walls of Chanute's taproom: the head of a Brown Wolf, the oven door from a gingerbread house, a cudgel-in-the-sack that jumped off the wall whenever a guest misbehaved, and, right above the bar and hanging from the chains with which he used to bind his victims, an arm of the Ogre who had ended Chanute's treasure-hunting days. The bluish skin still shimmered like a lizard's hide.

"Look who's here!" Chanute said, his grouchy mouth actually stretching into a smile. "I thought you were in Lotharaine, looking for an hourglass."

Chanute had been a legendary treasure hunter, but Jacob had meanwhile gained an equally famous reputation in that line of work, and the three men sitting at one of the stained tables curiously lifted their heads.

"Get rid of them!" Jacob whispered across the counter. "I have to talk to you."

Then he went up to the room that had for years now been the only place in either this world or the other that he could call home.

A wishing table, a glass slipper, the golden ball of a princess—Jacob had found many things in this world, and he had sold them for a lot of money to noblemen and rich merchants. But it was the chest behind the door of his simple room that held the treasures Jacob had kept for himself. These were the tools of his trade, though he had never thought they'd one day have to help him save his own brother.

The first item he took out of the chest was a hand-kerchief made of simple linen, but when it was rubbed between two fingers, it reliably produced one or two gold sovereigns. Jacob had received it years earlier from a Witch in exchange for a kiss that had burned his lips for weeks. The other items he packed into his knapsack looked just as innocuous: a silver snuffbox, a brass key, a tin plate, and a small bottle made of green glass. Each of these items had saved his life on more than one occasion.

When Jacob came back down the stairs, he found the taproom empty. Chanute was sitting at one of the tables. He pushed a mug of wine toward him as Jacob joined him.

"So? What kind of trouble are you in this time?" Chanute looked longingly at Jacob's wine; he only had a glass of water in front of him. In the past, he'd often been so drunk that Jacob had started hiding the bottles, though Chanute would always beat him for it. The old treasure hunter had often beaten Jacob, even when he was sober—until Jacob had one day pointed his own pistol at him. Chanute had also been drunk in the Ogre's cave. He would have probably kept his arm had he been able to see straight, but after that he had quit drinking. The treasure hunter had been a miserable replacement father, and Jacob was always on his guard with him, but if anyone knew what could save Will, then Albert Chanute most definitely did.

"What would you do if a friend of yours had been clawed by the Goyl?"

Chanute choked on his water and eyed him closely, as if to make sure Jacob was not talking about himself.

"I have no friends," he grunted. "And you don't, either. You have to trust friends, and neither of us is very good at that. So, who is it?"

Jacob shook his head.

"Of course. Jacob Reckless likes it mysterious. How could I forget?" Chanute's voice sounded bitter. Despite everything, he thought of Jacob as the son he had never had. "When did they get him?"

"Four days ago."

The Goyl had attacked them not far from a village where Jacob had been looking for the hourglass. He had underestimated how far their patrols were already venturing into imperial territory, and after Will had been clawed, he'd been in such pain that the journey back took them days. Back where? There was no "back" anymore, but Jacob had not had the courage yet to tell Will.

Chanute brushed his hand through his spiky hair. "Four days? Forget it. He's already half one of them.

You remember the time when the Empress was collecting all their colors? And that farmer tried to peddle us a dead moonstone he had covered in lamp soot as an onyx Goyl?"

Yes, Jacob remembered. The stone faces. That's what they were still called back then, and children were told stories about them to teach them to fear the night. When Chanute and he were still traveling together, the Goyl had only just begun to populate the caves aboveground, and every village used to organize Goyl hunts. But now they had a King, and he had turned the hunted into hunters.

There was a rustling near the back door, and Chanute drew his knife. He threw it so quickly that it nailed the rat in mid-jump against the wall.

"This world is going down the toilet," he growled, pushing back his chair. "Rats as big as dogs. The air on the street stinks like a Troll's cave from all the factories, and the Goyl are standing just a couple of miles from here."

He picked up the dead rat and threw it onto the table.

"There's nothing that helps against the petrified flesh. But if they'd gotten me, I'd ride to one of them Witches' houses and look in the garden for a bush with black berries." Chanute wiped the bloody knife on his sleeve. "It's got to be the garden of a child-eater, though."

"I thought the child-eating Witches all moved to Lotharaine since the other Witches started hunting them."

"But their houses are still there. The bush grows where they buried their leftovers. Those berries are the strongest antidote to curses I know of."

Witch-berries. Jacob looked at the oven door on the wall. "The Witch in the Hungry Forest was a child-eater, wasn't she?"

"One of the worst. I once looked in her house for one of them combs that you put into your hair and they turn you into a crow."

"I know. You sent me in there first."

"Really?" Chanute rubbed his fleshy nose. He'd convinced Jacob that the Witch had flown out.

"You poured liquor on my wounds." The imprints of her fingers were still visible on his throat. It had taken weeks for the burns to heal.

Jacob threw the knapsack over his shoulder. "I need a packhorse, some provisions, two rifles, and ammunition."

Chanute didn't seem to have heard Jacob. He was

staring at his trophies. "Good old times," he mumbled. "The Empress received me personally three times. How many audiences have you clocked up?"

Jacob closed his hand around the handkerchief in his pocket until he felt two gold sovereigns between his fingers.

"Two," he said, tossing the coins onto the table. He'd had six audiences with the Empress, but the lie made Chanute very happy.

"Put that gold away!" he growled. "I don't take no money from you." Then he held out his knife to Jacob.

"Here," he said. "There's nothing this blade won't cut. I have a feeling you'll need it more than I will."

6. Lovesick Fool

Will was gone. Jacob saw it immediately as he led the packhorse through the collapsed gate of the ruin. It lay as deserted as if his brother had never followed him through the mirror and all was fine and this world was still his, all his. For one moment he caught himself feeling relieved. *Let him go, Jacob.* Why not just forget he ever had a brother?

"He said he'd come back." Fox was sitting between the columns. The night turned her fur black. "I tried to stop him, but he's just as pigheaded as you."

Another mistake, Jacob. He should have taken Will with him to Schwanstein instead of hiding him here at the ruin. Will wanted to go home. Just go home. But he'd take the stone with him.

Jacob led the packhorse to the other two horses already grazing behind the ruin. He walked toward the tower. Its long shadow wrote a single word on the shattered flagstones: Back.

A threat for you, Jacob, but a promise for Will.

Ivy grew up the scorched walls so densely that its evergreen vines hung like a curtain over the doorway. The tower was the only part of the castle that had survived the fire nearly unscathed. The inside was swarming with bats, and the rope ladder Jacob had installed years earlier shimmered through the darkness. The Elves always left their dust on it as if to remind him that he had once come down here from another world.

Fox looked at him apprehensively as he reached for the ropes.

"We leave as soon as I get back with Will," Jacob said.

"Leave? For where?"

But Jacob was already climbing up the swaying ladder.

The tower room was bright with the light of the two moons, and his brother was standing next to the mirror. He was not alone.

The girl stepped out of his embrace as soon as she heard Jacob behind her. She was prettier than in the photos Will had shown him. *Lovesick fool.*

"What's she doing here?" Jacob felt his own rage like frost on his skin. "Have you lost your mind?"

Jacob brushed the elven dust from his hands. It worked like a sleeping potion if you weren't careful.

"Clara." Will took her hand. "This is my brother. Jacob."

He said her name as if he had pearls on his tongue. Will had always taken love too seriously.

"What else has to happen before you realize what kind of a place this is?" Jacob barked at him. "Send her back. Now."

She was afraid, though she tried hard to hide it. Afraid of the place that could not be, the red moon above her—*and of you, Jacob.* She seemed surprised he actually existed. Will's older brother, as unreal as the place she found herself in.

She took Will's blemished hand. "What is that?"

she asked in a halting voice as she stroked the stone. "I have never seen a skin condition like this."

Of course. A medical student....Look at her, Jacob! She's just as lovesick as your brother. So lovesick that she even followed him into a whole other world.

From the rafters above came a scraping sound, and a scrawny face peered down at them. The Stilt who had bitten Jacob on his first trip behind the mirror could not be driven from the tower, but its ugly face quickly disappeared behind the cobwebs as Jacob drew his pistol. For a while Jacob had borrowed guns from his father's collection, but at some point he'd had a gunsmith in New York put the workings of a modern pistol inside one of the old-fashioned shells.

Clara stared, dumbfounded, at the glinting muzzle.

"Send her back, Will." Jacob tucked the pistol back into his belt. "I won't tell you again."

Will had by now encountered things that were more frightening than a big brother, but finally he did turn around. He brushed the fair hair from Clara's forehead.

"He's right," Jacob heard Will whisper. "I'll come after you soon. It will heal. You'll see; my brother will find a way."

Jacob had never understood where all that trust

came from. Nothing had ever been able to shake it, not even all the years during which Will had barely seen him.

"Let's go." Jacob turned around and went toward the hatch.

"Go back, Clara. Please," he heard Will say.

But Jacob had already reached the bottom of the rope ladder by the time his brother finally caught up with him. Will climbed so slowly, it seemed he never wanted to reach the bottom. Then he stood there, looking at the elven dust on his hands. Deep sleep, enchanting dreams—not the worst gift, but Will wiped the dust from his fingers as Jacob had shown him. Then he touched his neck. The first traces of pale green were already showing there, too.

"You don't need anybody, right, Jake?" His voice nearly sounded envious. "You were always like that."

Jacob pushed aside the ivy.

"If you need her so much, you should leave her where she's safe."

"I just wanted to give her a call. She hadn't heard from me in weeks. I didn't think she'd follow me."

"Really? And what were you waiting for then up there?"

Will had no answer for that.

Fox was waiting by the horses, and she didn't like it at all that Jacob had brought Will back. *Nobody can help him.* Her gaze still said it.

We'll see, Fox.

The horses were agitated. Will soothingly patted their nostrils. His gentle brother. Will would always bring home every stray dog and cry bitter tears over the poisoned rats in the park. But what was growing in his flesh was anything but gentle.

"Where are we riding to?"

He looked up at the tower.

Jacob gave him one of the rifles from the panniers of the packhorse.

"To the Hungry Forest."

Fox lifted her head.

Yes, Fox, I know. Not a very pleasant place.

His mare shoved her head into his back. Jacob had paid Chanute a whole year's earnings for her, and she was worth every farthing. He tightened the strap on her saddle as Fox uttered a warning growl.

Steps. Hesitant. Then they stopped.

Jacob turned around.

"No matter what kind of place this is"—Clara was standing between the blackened columns—"I will not go back. Will needs me. And I want to know what happened."

Fox eyed her incredulously, like a strange animal. The women in her world wore long dresses and kept their hair pinned up or plaited, like peasant girls. This one was wearing trousers, and her hair was as short as a boy's.

The howl of a wolf pierced the darkness, and Will pulled Clara away. He talked at her, but she just took his arm and traced the stone veins in his skin with her fingers.

You're no longer the only one looking after Will, Jacob.

Clara looked at him, and her face briefly reminded Jacob of his mother. Why hadn't he ever told her about the mirror? What if the world behind it could have wiped at least some of the sadness off her face?

Too late, Jacob. Much too late.

Fox hadn't taken her eyes off the girl. Jacob sometimes forgot she was one, as well.

A second wolf howled. They were usually quite peaceful, but there was always a chance that there was a brown one among them, and those did like to eat human flesh.

Will listened anxiously into the night; then he again pleaded with Clara.

Fox lifted her muzzle. "We should leave," she whispered at Jacob.

"Not before he sends her back."

Fox looked at him. Eyes of pure amber.

"Take her along."

"No!"

She'd only slow them down. Fox knew as well as he that his brother was running out of time, though Jacob hadn't explained that to Will yet.

Fox turned.

"Take her along!" she said again. "Your brother will need her. And you will, too. Or don't you trust my nose anymore?"

With that, she disappeared into the night as if she was tired of waiting for him.

7. The House of the Witch

A thicket of roots, thorns, and leaves. Giant trees, and saplings stretching toward what scant light trickled through the thick canopy. Swarms of will-o'-the-wisps above putrid ponds, and clearings where toadstools drew their poisonous circles. Jacob had last been in the Hungry Forest four months earlier, to find a Man-Swan wearing a shirt of nettles over his feathers. But

after three days he'd abandoned the search, for he had not been able to breathe under the dark trees.

It took them until midday to reach the edge of the forest, because Will had been in pain again. The stone had now spread all over his neck, though Clara pretended not to see it. Love makes you blind—she seemed intent on proving that proverb. She never budged from Will's side; she wrapped her arms around him whenever the stone grew a little further and he doubled over in the saddle with pain. But when she felt unobserved, Jacob saw his own fear on her face. When she asked him what he knew about the stone, he gave her the same lies he had given his brother: that it was only Will's skin that was changing, and that it would be simple enough to heal him in this world. She hadn't taken much convincing. Both she and Will were only too happy to believe whatever comforting lies he told them.

Clara rode better than he'd expected. Jacob had bought her a dress from a market they had passed along the way, but she made him swap it for a man's clothes after trying in vain to mount her horse in the wide skirt. A girl in men's clothes, and the stone on Will's skin—Jacob was glad when they finally left the villages and highways behind and could ride under the trees, even though he knew what would be awaiting there.

Barkbiters, Mushroom-Wights, Trappers, Crow-Men. The Hungry Forest had many unpleasant inhabitants, though the Empress had been trying for years to clear it of its terrors. Despite the dangers, there was a lively trade in horns, teeth, skins, and other body parts of the Hungry Forest's creatures. Jacob had never earned his money that way, but there were many who made quite a decent living of it: fifteen silver dollars for a Mushroom-Wight (a two-dollar bonus if it spat real fly-agaric poison), thirty for a Barkbiter (not a lot, considering the hunt could easily leave the hunter dead), and forty for a Crow-Man (who at least only went for the eyes).

Many trees were already shedding their leaves, but the canopy above them was still so dense that the day beneath it dissolved into a checkered autumnal twilight. They soon had to start leading the horses on foot, for they kept getting caught in the thorny undergrowth. Jacob had instructed Will and Clara not to touch the trees. However, the shimmering pearls that a Barkbiter had left sprouting as bait on an oak limb made Clara forget his warnings. Jacob barely managed to pluck the foul creature from her wrist before it could crawl up her sleeve.

"This here," he said, holding the Barkbiter in front of Clara's face, close enough for her to see the sharp teeth above the scabbed lips, "is just one of the reasons why you shouldn't touch the trees. His first bite will make you drowsy. A second one, and you'll be completely paralyzed. But you will still be fully conscious while his entire clan starts to gorge itself on your blood. Trust me, it's not a pleasant way to die."

Do you see now that you should have sent her back? Will read the reproach on Jacob's face as he pulled Clara to his side. But from then on she was careful. It was Clara who pulled back Will in time when she saw the glistening net of a Trapper stretched across their path, and it was she who shooed away the Gold-Ravens trying to squawk dark curses into their ears.

*And yet....*She belonged here even less than his brother did.

Fox gave him a look.

Stop it, her eyes said. *She is here, and I am telling you again: He will need her.*

Fox. His furry shadow. The will-o'-the-wisps, drifting in thick iridescent swarms among the trees, had often led even Jacob astray with their alluring hum. But

Fox just shook them from her fur like troublesome flies and ran on unwaveringly.

After three hours, the first Witch's tree appeared between the oak and ash trees, and Jacob was just about to warn Will and Clara about their branches and how they loved to poke at human eyes, when Fox suddenly stopped.

The faint sound was nearly drowned out by the hum of the will-o'-the-wisps. It sounded like the snip-snap of a pair of scissors. Not a terribly threatening sound, and Will and Clara didn't even notice it. But the vixen's fur bristled, and Jacob put his hand on his saber. He knew of only one creature in this forest that made such a sound, and it was the only one he definitely did not want to run into.

"Let's get a move on," he whispered to Fox. "How much farther to the house?"

Snip-snap. It was coming closer.

"It's going to be tight," Fox whispered back.

The snipping stopped, but the sudden silence was no less ominous. No bird sang. Even the will-o'-the-wisps had vanished. Fox cast a worried glance at the trees before she scampered ahead again, so briskly that the horses barely managed to keep up with her through the dense undergrowth.

The forest was growing darker, and Jacob pulled from his saddlebag the flashlight he had brought from another world. More and more often they now had to skirt around Witch's trees. Hawthorn took the place of ash and oak. Pines sucked up the scant light with their black-green needles, and the horses shied when they saw the house appear between the trees.

When Jacob had come here some years earlier with Chanute, the red roof tiles had shone through the undergrowth so brightly, it had looked as if the Witch had painted them with cherry juice. Now they were covered in moss, and the paint was peeling off the window frames. But there were still a few pieces of gingerbread stuck to the walls and the steep roof. Sugary icicles hung from the gutters and the window-sills, and the whole house smelled of honey and cinnamon—as befitted a trap for children. The Witches had tried many times to banish the child-eaters from their clans, and two years ago they had finally declared war on them. The Witch who had plagued the Hungry Forest was now supposedly living out her life as a warty toad in some silty pool.

The wrought-iron fence that surrounded her house still had some colorful candy stuck to it. Jacob's mare trembled as he led her through the gate. The fence of a gingerbread house would admit anyone but would not let anybody out. During their visit, Chanute had taken care to leave the gate wide open, but now Jacob was more worried about what was following them than about the abandoned house. As he closed the gate behind Will, the snipping could again be heard clearly, and this time it sounded almost angry. But at least it didn't come any closer. Fox shot Jacob a relieved glance. It was just as they had hoped: Their pursuer had been no friend of the Witch.

"But what if he waits for us?" Fox whispered.

Yes, what then, Jacob? He did not care, just as long as the bush Chanute had described to him was still growing behind the house.

Will had led the horses to the well and lowered the rusty pail to draw water for them. He eyed the gingerbread house as if it were a poisonous plant. Clara, however, was running her fingers over the icing as if she could not believe what she saw.

Nibble, nibble, little mouse, who's been nibbling at my house?

Which version of the story had Clara heard?

Then she took hold of Hansel with her bony hand, carried him away to a little hutch with a barred door, and shut him up there. He could shout all he liked, but it did him no good.

"Take care she doesn't eat any of the cakes," Jacob said to Fox. Then he set off in search of the berries.

Behind the house the nettles were growing so high, it looked as if they were standing guard over the Witch's garden. They burnt Jacob's skin, but he beat a path through their poisonous leaves until he found what he was looking for between the hemlock and the deadly nightshade: a nondescript little bush with feathered leaves. Jacob was filling his hand with its black berries when he heard footsteps.

Clara was standing between the overgrown plots.

"Monkshood, May lilies, hemlock." She looked at him, puzzled. "These are all poisonous plants."

She had obviously learned a few useful things as a premed student. Will had already told Jacob a dozen times how he had met her at the hospital, in the ward where their mother had been treated. *When you were not there, Jacob.*

He got to his feet. Out in the forest, the sound of snipping could be heard again.

"Sometimes it takes a poison to heal," he said. "I'm sure I don't have to tell you that. Though I doubt you've ever learned about these berries."

He filled her hands with the shiny black fruit.

"Will must eat at least a dozen of them. They should have done their work by the time the sun rises. Persuade him to lie down in the house; he hasn't slept in days."

Goyl didn't need much sleep. One of the many advantages they had over humans.

Clara looked at the berries in her hand. She had a thousand questions on her tongue, but she didn't ask them. What had Will told her about him? *"Yes, I do have a brother. But he's been a stranger to me for a long time now."*

She turned around and listened to the forest. This time she'd heard the snipping as well.

"What is that?" she asked.

"They call him the Tailor. He doesn't dare to cross the Witch's fence, but we cannot leave as long as he's there. I'll try to drive him off." From his pocket he pulled the key he had taken from the chest in Chanute's tavern. "The fence won't let you leave. But this key opens every door. I'll throw it over the gate once I'm out, just in case I don't come back. Fox will lead you back to the tower. But don't unlock the gate before it gets light."

Will was still standing by the well. He stumbled with fatigue as he walked toward Clara.

"Don't let him sleep in the room with the oven," Jacob muttered into Clara's ear. "The air there gives bleak dreams. And make sure he doesn't try to follow me."

Will ate the berries without hesitation. The magic that would heal everything. Even as a child he had believed in such things much more readily than Jacob. It was obvious how tired he was, and he didn't protest when Clara led him toward the gingerbread house. The sun was setting behind the trees, and the red moon hung above the treetops like a bloody fingerprint. When the sun returned, the stone in his brother's skin would be nothing but a bad dream. If the berries worked.

If.

Jacob went to the fence and stared out into the forest.

Snip-snap.

Their pursuer was still there.

Fox's eyes followed Jacob anxiously as he walked toward the mare and pulled Chanute's knife from the saddlebag. Bullets were useless against the one who was waiting for him outside. It was said they even made the Tailor stronger.

A thousand shadows filled the forest, and Jacob believed he could see a dark figure standing among the trees. *He'll at least help pass the time until sunrise, Jacob.* He pushed the knife into his belt and took the flashlight from his knapsack. Fox ran after him as he approached the fence.

"You can't go out there. It's getting dark."

"And?"

"Maybe he'll be gone by morning!"

"Why should he?"

The gate sprang open as soon as Jacob pushed the key into the rusty lock.

So many desperate children must have rattled this gate in vain.

"Stay here, Fox," he said.

But as he closed the gate behind him, she quietly slipped out by his side.

8. CLARA

The first room was the one with the oven, but Clara pulled Will along as he looked through the door. The narrow corridor smelled of cakes and roasted almonds, and in the next room a shawl, embroidered with a pattern of black birds, was draped over the back of a tattered armchair. The bed was in the last room. It was barely big enough for both of them, and the

blankets were moth-eaten, but Will was already fast asleep by the time Jacob pulled the gate shut outside.

The growing stone traced patterns on Will's neck, just as the dappled sun had in the forest. Clara carefully touched the pale green. So cool and smooth. So beautiful, yet so terrible.

What would happen if the berries didn't work? Will's brother knew the answer, and it frightened him, though he was very good at hiding it.

Jacob. Will had told Clara about him, but he had only ever shown her one photograph, and in it they had both still been children. Even back then Jacob's gaze had been different from his brother's. There was none of Will's gentleness to be found there. None of his stillness.

Clara extricated herself from Will's embrace and covered him with the Witch's blanket. A moth had landed on his shoulder, black, like an imprint of the night. It fluttered away as Clara bent over Will to kiss him. He did not wake up, and she left him alone and stepped outside.

The house covered in cakes, the red moon over the trees—everything she saw seemed so unreal that she felt like a sleepwalker. Everything she knew was gone. Everything she remembered seemed lost. Will was the only familiar thing, but the strangeness was already growing on his skin.

The vixen wasn't there. Of course. She'd gone with Jacob. The key was right next to the gate, just as he had promised. Clara picked it up and ran her fingers over the engraved metal.

The voices of the will-o'-the-wisps filled the air like the hum of bees. A raven cawed somewhere in the trees. But Clara was listening for another sound: the sharp snipping that had darkened Jacob's face with worry and had made him go back into the forest. What was waiting out there, turning even the house of a child-eater into a safe haven?

Snip-snap. There it was again. Like the snapping of metallic teeth. Clara backed away from the fence. Long shadows were growing toward the house, and she felt the same fear she'd felt as a child when she was alone and heard steps in the hallway.

She should have told Will what his brother was planning. He would never forgive her if Jacob didn't come back.

He would come back.

He had to come back.

They'd never find their way home without him.

9. THE TAILOR

Was he coming after them? Jacob walked slowly, so the hunter he was trying to lure could follow. But all he heard were his own steps, rotting twigs snapping under his boots, leaves rustling as he pushed through the undergrowth. Where was he? Jacob was beginning to fear that their pursuer had forgotten his wariness of the Witch and was sneaking through the gate

behind his back, when suddenly he heard the snipping again, coming through the forest to his left. It was just as everybody said: The Tailor loved to play a little cat and mouse with his victims before commencing his bloody work.

Nobody could say who or what exactly the Tailor was. The stories about him were just about as old as the Hungry Forest itself. There was only one thing everybody knew for certain: that the Tailor had earned his name by tailoring his clothes from human skin.

Snip-snap, clip-clip. The trees opened into a clearing. Fox gave Jacob a warning look as a murder of crows fluttered up from the branches of an oak. The snip-snap grew so loud that it drowned out their squawks, and under an oak the beam of Jacob's flashlight found the outline of a man.

The Tailor did not like the probing finger of light. He uttered an angry grunt and swatted at it as if it were an annoying bug. But Jacob let the light explore further, over the bearded, dirt-caked face, the gruesome clothes, which at first sight simply looked like poorly tanned leather, and on to the gross hands with which the Tailor plied his bloody trade. The fingers on his left hand ended in broad blades, each as long as a dagger. The blades on the right were just as long and lethal, though these were slender and pointed, like giant sewing needles. Both hands were missing a finger—obviously other victims had tried to defend their skins—though the Tailor did not seem to miss them much. He let his murderous fingernails slice through the air as if he were cutting a pattern from the shadows of the trees, taking measurements for the clothes he would soon fashion from Jacob's skin.

Fox bared her teeth and retreated with a growl to Jacob's side.

Jacob shooed her behind him. He drew his saber with his left hand and Chanute's knife with his right.

His opponent moved clumsily, like a bear, though his hands cut through the thickets of thistles with terrifying zeal. His eyes were blank, like those of a dead man, but the bearded face was contorted into a mask of bloodlust, and he bared his yellow teeth as if he wanted to peel the skin off Jacob's flesh with them.

At first the Tailor hacked at him with the broad blades. Jacob deflected them with his saber while he slashed at the needle hand with his knife. He'd fought a half dozen drunk soldiers, the guards of enchanted castles, highwaymen, and even a pack of trained wolves, but this was far worse. The Tailor's hacking and stabbing were so relentless, Jacob felt as if he were caught in a threshing machine.

His foe wasn't very tall, and Jacob was more nimble, yet soon he felt the first cuts on his arms and shoulders. *Come on, Jacob. Look at his clothes. Do you want to end up like that?* He hacked off one of the needle fingers with his knife, used the ensuing howls of rage to catch his breath—and barely managed to yank up his saber before the blades could slash his face. Two of the needles cut his cheek like the claws of a cat. A third nearly pierced his arm. Jacob retreated between the trees, letting the blades cut into the bark and not his skin. But the Tailor freed himself again and again and didn't seem to tire, while Jacob's arms grew ever heavier.

He cut off another finger as one of the blades hacked into the bark right next to him. The Tailor howled like a wolf, yet he slashed at him with even greater rage—and there was no blood running from his wounds.

You will end up as a pair of pants! Jacob's breathing grew labored. His heart was racing. He stumbled over a root, and before he could catch himself, the Tailor stabbed one of his needles deep into Jacob's shoulder. The pain buckled his knees, and he had no breath left to call Fox back as she jumped at the Tailor and sunk her teeth deep into his leg. She had so often saved Jacob's skin, but never quite so literally. The Tailor tried to shake her off. He had forgotten about Jacob, and as he angrily struck out to hack his blades into her furry body, Jacob slashed off his left arm with Chanute's knife.

The Tailor's scream echoed through the dark forest. He stared at the useless stump of his arm and at the bladed hand lying on the moss in front of him. Then he spun around, wheezing, to face Jacob. The remaining hand came down on Jacob with deadly force. Three steel needles, murderous daggers. Jacob thought he could already feel their metal inside him, but before they could pierce his flesh, he rammed his knife deep into the Tailor's chest.

The Tailor grunted, pressing his fingers to his terrible shirt. Then his knees buckled.

Jacob staggered to the nearest tree, fighting for breath while the Tailor thrashed in pain on the wet moss. One final gasp and then silence. Jacob did not drop his knife, even though the glazed eyes stared emptily skyward out of the grimy face. He wasn't convinced there was such a thing as death for the Tailor.

Fox shivered as if the hounds had been after her.

Jacob let himself drop to his knees next to her and stared at the now lifeless body of the Tailor. Jacob had no idea how long he remained crouched there. His skin was burning as if he'd been rolling around in broken glass. His shoulder was numb with pain, and in front of his eyes the blades were still performing their murderous dance.

"Jacob!" Fox's voice seemed to come to him from afar. "Get up. It's safer at the house!"

He got to his feet.

The Tailor still wasn't moving.

The journey back to the gingerbread house seemed very long, and when it finally appeared between the trees, Jacob saw Clara waiting behind the fence.

"Oh, God!" was all she murmured when she saw the blood on his shirt. She fetched water from the well and washed the cuts. Jacob flinched as her fingers probed his shoulder.

"This one is deep," she said as Fox anxiously crouched by her side. "I wish it would bleed more freely."

"There's iodine and some bandages in my saddlebag." Jacob was grateful that she was used to the sight of bloody wounds. "What about Will? Is he asleep?"

"Yes." And the stone was still there. She didn't have to say it.

Jacob could see from the expression on her face that she wanted to know what had happened in the forest, but that was the last thing he wanted to remember.

Clara fetched the iodine from his saddlebag and dripped the tincture on his wound, but she still looked worried.

"Fox, what plants do you usually roll in when you're wounded?" she asked.

The vixen showed her some herbs in the Witch's garden. They gave off a bittersweet aroma as Clara plucked them apart and pressed them against Jacob's pierced skin.

"Like a born Witch," he said. "I thought Will said he met you in a hospital."

She smiled. It made her look very young.

"In our world, the Witches work in hospitals. Remember?"

Clara noticed the scars on Jacob's back as she pulled the shirt over his bandaged shoulder. "How did those happen? Must have been terrible injuries."

Fox shot him a knowing look, but Jacob just buttoned his shirt with a shrug.

"I survived."

Clara looked at him pensively.

"Thank you," she said. "For whatever you did out there. I'm so glad you came back."

10. Fur and Skin

Jacob knew too much about gingerbread houses
to be able to find any sleep under the sugar-icing
roof. He took the tin plate from his saddlebag
and sat down with it in front of the well, polish-
ing it until it filled with bread and cheese. It
wasn't a five-course dinner, like the one provided
by the wishing table he had found for the Empress,
but at least the plate could fit into a saddlebag.

The red moon splashed rust into the night, and dawn was still hours away, but Jacob didn't dare go see whether the stone in Will's skin had vanished. Fox sat down next to him and licked her fur. The Tailor had kicked her, and she had several cuts on her body, but she was all right. Human skin was so much more fragile than fur—or Goyl skin.

"You should try to sleep," she said.

"I can't sleep."

Jacob's shoulder ached, and he imagined he could feel the Witch's black magic battling the Dark Fairy's spell.

"What are you going to do if the berries do work? Take them back?"

Fox tried hard to sound unconcerned, but Jacob heard the unspoken question behind her words. No matter how often he told Fox how much he liked her world, she never lost the fear that one day he would climb up the tower and never return.

"Of course," he said. "And they'll live happily ever after."

"What about us?" Fox snuggled against him as he shuddered in the cold night air. "Winter's coming. We could go south, to Granady or Lombardia, and look for the hourglass."

The hourglass that stopped time. Just a few weeks back, it had been all Jacob could think about. The talking mirror. The glass slipper. The spinning wheel that spun gold. There was always something he could hunt for in this world. And most of the time it helped him forget that he had never been able to find the one thing he really wanted.

Jacob took a piece of bread from the plate and offered it to Fox. "When did you last shift?" he asked as she greedily snapped at it.

She tried to scamper away, but he grabbed her fur. "Fox!"

She tried to bite his hand, but then the fox-shaped shadow, cast by the moonlight on the wall of the well, began to stretch, and Jacob felt himself pushed away by the strong hands of a girl kneeling next to him.

Her hair was as red as the pelt she so much preferred to her human skin. It fell down her back so long and thick that it looked almost as though she were still wearing her fur. Even the russet dress that covered her freckled skin glistened in the moonlight like the coat of a fox. Its fabric seemed to have been woven from the same silky hair.

She had grown up in these past months, nearly as suddenly as a fox cub becomes a vixen. But Jacob still saw the ten-year-old girl he had found one night, crying at the bottom of the tower because he had stayed much longer in the world he had come from than he had promised. She had been following Jacob for nearly a year by then, without ever showing him her human form. He kept reminding her that she would one day lose her human form if she kept wearing her fur too long, even though he knew that, should Fox ever be forced to decide, she would always choose the fur. At the age of seven she had saved a wounded vixen from her two elder brothers and their sticks, and the next day she had found the furry dress on her bed. It had given her the body she had come to regard as her true self, and Fox's greatest fear was that someday someone might steal the dress and take the fur away from her.

Jacob leaned back against the well. *It will be all right, Jacob.* But the night seemed endless. He felt Fox lean her head against his shoulder, and finally he fell asleep, next to the girl who did not want the skin that his brother had to fight for. He slept fitfully and even his dreams turned into stone. Chanute, the paperboy on the square, his mother, his father...they all froze into statues standing among the trees next to the dead Tailor.

"Jacob! Wake up!"

Fox was wearing her fur again. The first light of dawn was seeping through the pine trees. Jacob's shoulder ached so much, he barely managed to get to his feet. *All will be well, Jacob. Chanute knows this world like no one else. Remember how he exorcised the Witch's spell from you? You were already half-dead. And the Stilt bite? And his recipe against Waterman venom?*

His heart beat faster with every step he took toward the gingerbread house.

The sweet smell inside nearly choked him. It was probably the reason that Will and Clara were still fast asleep. She had her arms wrapped around Will, whose face was so peaceful, as if he were sleeping in the bed of a prince, not a child-eater. But his left cheek was speckled with jade, as if it had spilled onto his skin, and the nails on his left hand were nearly as black as the claws that had sown the petrified flesh into his shoulder.

How loud a heart could beat. Until it took your breath away.

All will be well.

Jacob was still standing there, staring at the stone, when Will finally stirred.

Jacob's eyes told him everything. Will put his hand to his neck and traced the stone up to his cheek.

Think, Jacob! But his mind had drowned in the fear that was flooding his brother's face.

They let Clara sleep. Will followed Jacob outside like a sleepwalker caught in a nightmare.

Fox backed away from him. The look she gave Jacob said only one thing.

Lost.

And that was how Will stood there. Lost. He touched his disfigured face, and for the first time Jacob no longer saw there any of the trust his brother usually gave so freely. Instead, he believed he saw all the blame he put on himself. All the *If only you'd been more careful, Jacob.... If you only hadn't taken him so far east.... If only...*

Will stepped to the window behind which the oven stood, and he stared at the image the dark panes threw back at him.

Jacob, however, was looking at the soot-blackened cobwebs under the sugared roof. They reminded him of other webs, just as dark, spun to catch the night.

What an idiot he was. What was he doing at a Witch's house? This was the curse of a Fairy. *A Fairy!*

Fox looked at him with apprehension.

"No!" she barked.

Sometimes she knew what he was thinking even before he did.

"She will definitely be able to help him. After all, she is her sister."

"You can't go back to her! Ever."

Will turned around.

"Go back to whom?"

Jacob didn't answer. He reached for the medallion beneath his shirt. His fingers still remembered picking the petal that he kept inside it. Just as his heart remembered the one from whom the leaf protected him.

"Go and wake Clara," he said to Will. "We're leaving. All will be well."

It was a long way—four days, maybe more—and they had to be faster than the stone.

Fox was still looking at him.

No, Jacob. No! her eyes pleaded with him.

Of course she remembered it all as well as he did, if not better.

Fear, rage, lost time. "*Must have been terrible injuries.*"

But this was the only way, if he wanted to keep his brother.

11. Hentzau

The Man-Goyl whom Hentzau found in a deserted coach station was growing a skin of malachite. Half of his face was already grained with dark green. Hentzau let him go, like all the others they had found, with the advice to seek refuge in the nearest Goyl camp—before his own kind could murder him. But there was no gold yet in his eyes, only the memory that

his skin had not always been made of malachite. He ran away as if there were still someplace he could run to. Hentzau shuddered at the thought that the Fairy might one day sow human flesh into his jasper skin.

Malachite, bloodstone, jasper. Hentzau and his soldiers had even found the color of the King, but of course no trace of the stone they were looking for.

Jade.

Old women wore it as talismans around their necks, and they secretly knelt before idols carved from the holy stone. Mothers sewed it into their children's clothes so the stone would make them fearless and protect them. But there had never been a Goyl whose skin was made of jade.

How long would the Dark Fairy have him search? How long would he have to look a fool in front of his soldiers, the King, and himself? What if she had invented the dream only to separate him from Kami'en? And off he'd run, ever loyal and obedient, like a dog.

Hentzau looked down the deserted road, which vanished between the trees. His soldiers were growing nervous. The Goyl avoided the Hungry Forest as much as the humans did. The Fairy knew that very well. This was a game. Yes, that's what it was. Nothing but a game. And he was tired of being her dog.

The moth settled on Hentzau's chest just as he was about to give the order to mount up. It clawed itself to his gray uniform, right above where his heart was beating, and Hentzau saw the Man-Goyl just as clearly as the Fairy had in her dreams.

The jade ran through his human skin like a promise. It could not be.

And then the deep brought forth a King, and when there came a time of great peril for him, there also came the Jade Goyl, born from glass and silver, and he made the King invincible, even to death.

Old wives' tales. As a child, Hentzau had loved nothing more than listening to them, because they gave the world meaning and a happy ending. A world that was clearly divided into above and below and that was ruled by soft-fleshed gods. But since then he had sliced their soft flesh and had learned that they weren't gods, just as he had learned that the world made no sense and that there were no happy endings.

But there he was. Hentzau saw him clearly, as clearly as if he could have reached out and touched the pale green stone that had already spilled onto the Man-Goyl's cheek.

The Jade Goyl. Born from the curse of the Fairy.

Had this been her plan all along? Had she sown all that petrified flesh only to reap him?

What do you care, Hentzau? Find him!

The moth spread its wings, and he saw the fields he had fought on just a few months earlier. Fields that bordered the eastern boundary of the Hungry Forest. He was searching on the wrong side.

Hentzau suppressed a curse and swatted the moth dead.

His soldiers looked at him in surprise when he gave the order to ride east again, but they were relieved he didn't lead them deeper into the forest. Hentzau wiped the crushed wings from his uniform as he swung himself into the saddle. None of them had seen the moth, and they would all confirm that he had found the Jade Goyl without the Fairy's help—just as he kept telling everyone that it was Kami'en who was winning the war, and not the spell of his immortal beloved.

Jade.

She had dreamed the truth.

Or had turned a dream into truth.

12. His Own Kind

It was early afternoon by the time they finally left the forest. Dark clouds hung above fields and meadows, patches of green, yellow, and brown that stretched to the horizon. Elderberry bushes bore heavy clusters of black berries, and Elves, their wings wet with rain, fluttered among the wildflowers by the roadside. However, the farms they passed were all

deserted, and on the fields cannons were rusting among the unharvested wheat.

Jacob was grateful for all the abandoned farms, for by now it would have been perfectly obvious to anyone looking at Will what was growing in his flesh. It had been raining on and off since they had come out of the forest, and the green stone on his face shimmered like the glaze of some sinister potter.

Jacob had still not told Will where he was leading him, and he was glad that Will didn't ask. It was already enough that Fox knew that their destination was the only place in this world he had sworn never to return to.

Soon the rain was falling so mercilessly that even the vixen's fur no longer gave her any protection. Jacob's shoulder throbbed with every movement, as if the Tailor were jabbing his needles into it again, but with every glance at Will's face, Jacob pushed away any thought of rest. They were running out of time.

Maybe it was the pain that made him careless. He barely noticed the abandoned farm when it appeared by the side of the road, and Fox only caught the scent when it was already too late. Eight men, ragged but armed. They suddenly emerged from one of the dilapidated barns and had their rifles trained on the

travelers before Jacob could draw his pistol. Two of
the men were wearing imperial tunics, and a third the
gray jacket of a Goyl soldier. Plunderers and desert-
ers. The human debris of war. Two more had hung
on their belts the same trophies imperial soldiers liked
to display: the fingers of their stone-skinned enemies,
in all the colors they could find.

For one brief moment, Jacob hoped they wouldn't
notice the stone. Because of the rain, Will had drawn
the hood of his coat well over his face. However, one
of them, a scrawny weasel of a man, noticed the
infected hand as he dragged Will from his horse, and
he yanked the hood off his head.

Clara attempted to shield him, but the one with
the Goyl jacket pushed her out of the way, and Will's
face turned into that of a stranger. Never before had
Jacob seen in his brother's features such a powerful
desire to hurt someone. Will struggled to free himself, but the weasel punched him in the face, and
when Jacob's hand went for his pistol, their leader
quickly put the muzzle of his rifle to Jacob's chest.

He was a heavyset fellow with only three fingers on
his left hand. His threadbare jacket was covered with
the semiprecious stones Goyl officers wore on their
collars to denote their rank. There was a lot of booty

to be grabbed on the battlefields once the living left the dead behind.

"Why haven't you shot that Man-Goyl yet?" the leader asked while he searched Jacob's pockets. "Haven't you heard? There are no more rewards to be had for his lot, now that they've started negotiating with them."

He pulled out Jacob's handkerchief but shoved it back heedlessly before a gold sovereign could drop into his calloused hand. Behind them, Fox scurried into the ruined stable. Jacob could feel Clara looking at him pleadingly, but what did she expect? That he could take on eight men at once?

Threefingers poured out the contents of Jacob's purse and gave a disappointed grunt when all he found were a few copper coins. The others, however, were still staring at Will. They were going to kill him. Just for kicks. And put his fingers on their belts. *Do something, Jacob! But what?*

Talk, play for time, wait for a miracle.

"I am taking him to someone who will give him back his skin." The rain was running down his face, and the weasel was jabbing his rifle into Will's side. *Keep talking, Jacob!* "He's my brother. Let us go, and in a week's time I'll be back with a sack of gold."

"Sure!" Threefingers nodded to the others. "Take them behind the barn, and shoot this one in the head. I like his clothes."

Jacob pushed away the two men who reached out to grab him, but a third put a knife to his throat. The man was wearing the clothes of a peasant. They hadn't always been robbers.

"What are you talking about?" he hissed into Jacob's ear. "Nothing can give them their skin back. I shot my own son when the moonstone started growing on his forehead!"

The blade was pushed against his throat with such ferocity that Jacob could barely breathe.

"It's the curse of the Dark Fairy!" he croaked. "So I'm taking him to her sister. She'll break it."

How they all stared at him. Fairy. Just a word. Five letters, which contained all the magic and all the terror of this world.

The pressure on the knife eased a little, but the face of the man was still contorted with rage and helpless grief. Jacob was tempted to ask him how old his son had been.

"Nobody just goes to see a Fairy." The boy who stammered these words was fifteen at the most. "They come and get you."

"I know a way." *Keep talking, Jacob.* "I've been there before."

"Really? So why aren't you dead, then?" The knife was breaking his skin. "Or crazy, like the ones who come back and then drown themselves in the nearest pond?"

Jacob felt Will looking at him. What was he thinking? That his older brother was telling fairy tales, just as he had done when they were young and Will couldn't sleep?

"She will help him," he said again, hoarse from the pressure of the knife. *But before that, you'll kill us. And it still won't bring back your son.*

The weasel pushed the muzzle of his rifle into Will's blotched cheek. "Going to see the Fairies? Can't you see he's making fun of you, Stanis? Let's just shoot them already!"

He shoved Will toward the barn. Two of the others grabbed Clara. *Now, Jacob. What have you got to lose?* But Threefingers suddenly spun around and stared past the stables to the south. Through the rain came the snorting of horses.

Riders.

They came over the fallow fields on horses that

were as gray as their uniforms, and Will's face said very clearly who they were, even before the weasel yelled it to the others.

"Goyl!"

The peasant pointed his rifle at Will, as if only he could have called them, but Jacob shot him before the man could pull the trigger. Three of the Goyl, riding at full gallop, drew their sabers. They still preferred fighting with their swords, though their battles were now won with guns. Clara stared, dumbfounded, at the stone faces—and then she looked at Jacob. *Yes, that's what he's becoming. You still love him now?*

The bandits sought cover behind a toppled cart. They had clearly forgotten about their prisoners, and Jacob quickly pushed Will and Clara toward the horses.

"Fox!" he yelled, grabbing the mare's reins. Where was she?

Two of the Goyl fell off their horses; the others took cover behind the barn. Threefingers was a good shot.

Clara was already sitting on her horse, but Will was just standing there, staring across the yard at the Goyl.

"Get on your horse, Will!" Jacob screamed as he swung himself onto his mare.

But his brother didn't stir.

Jacob was about to drive his horse toward Will when he saw Fox scamper out of the barn. She was hobbling, and Jacob saw the weasel aim his rifle at her. He shot the man down, but just as he reined in the mare and leaned forward to grab Fox by her nape, he was hit on his injured shoulder by the butt of a rifle. The boy. He was standing there, holding his empty rifle by the barrel. He was already striking out again, as if by killing Jacob he could slay his own fear. The pain made everything swim in front of Jacob's eyes. He managed to draw his pistol, but the Goyl were quicker. They swarmed out from behind the barn, and one of their bullets hit the boy in the back.

Jacob grabbed Fox and lifted her into the saddle. Will had also swung himself back onto his horse, though he was still staring at the Goyl.

"Will!" Jacob yelled again. "Ride, dammit!"

His brother didn't even look at him.

"Will!" Clara screamed, glancing desperately at the fighting men.

But Will only came to when Jacob snatched his reins.

"Ride!" he barked at Will once more. "Ride, and don't look back."

And at last his brother turned his horse.

13. Of the Use of Daughters

Defeated. Therese of Austry was standing by the window, staring down at the palace guards. They were patrolling in front of the gate as if nothing had happened. The whole city lay below her as if nothing had happened. But she had lost a war. For the first time. And every night she dreamed she was drowning in bloody

water, which invariably turned into the pale red stone-skin of her foe.

For the past half hour, her ministers and generals had been explaining to her why she had lost. They were all in her audience chamber, decorated with the medals she'd given them, and they tried to put the blame on her. "The Goyl rifles are better." "They have faster trains." But she knew this war was being won by the King with the carnelian skin because he had a better grasp of strategy than all of them together. And because he had a mistress who, for the first time in more than three hundred years, had put the magic of the Fairies in the service of a King.

A carriage drew up to the gate, and three Goyl climbed out. They acted so civilized. They weren't even in uniform. How she would have loved to order her guards to drag them through the courtyard and club them to death, as her grandfather would have done. But these were different times. Now it was the Goyl who did the clubbing. They would sit down with her counselors, sip tea from silver cups, and negotiate terms of surrender. The guards opened the gate, and the Empress turned her back to the window as the Goyl crossed the courtyard.

They were still talking, all her useless, medaled

generals, while her ancestors stared down at her from the golden, silk-draped walls. Right next to the door was a portrait of her father, gaunt and upright, like a stork, continuously at war with his royal brother from Lotharaine, just as she had been fighting his son, Crookback, for years. Next to him was her grandfather, who, like the Goyl King, had once had an affair with a Fairy. His yearning for her had finally driven him to drown himself in the royal lily pond. He'd had himself portrayed on a Unicorn, for which his favorite horse was the model, with a narwhal horn attached to its head. It looked ludicrous, and the Empress had always preferred the painting next to his. That one showed her great-grandfather with his elder brother, who had been disinherited because he had taken his alchemical experiments too seriously. Her father had always been outraged by that painting because the painter had caught his great-uncle's blind eyes so realistically. As a child, she would push a chair under the picture, climbing up to get a closer look at the scars around those empty eyes. He'd supposedly been blinded by an experiment in which he had tried to turn his own heart into gold, and yet of all her ancestors, he was the only one who was smiling—which had always made her think that his experiment must have been successful and that he indeed had a golden heart beating in his chest.

Men. All of them. Crazy or sane, but always men. For centuries only men had ascended to the throne of Austry—and that had changed only because her father had sired four daughters but not a single son.

She, too, had no son, just a daughter. But she had never intended to turn her into a bargaining chip, as her father had done with her younger sisters. One for King Crookback, in his gloomy castle in Lotharaine; one for her cousin in Albion, the obsessive huntsman; and the youngest bartered away to some eastern potentate who had already buried two wives.

No. She had wanted to put her daughter on the throne, see her portrait on that wall, framed in gold, between all those men. Amalie of Austry, daughter of Therese, who had once dreamed of being called The Great. But there was no other way, or they would both drown in that bloody water—she, her daughter, her people, her throne, this city, and the whole country, together with those idiots who were still holding forth about why they hadn't been able to win the war for her. Therese's father would have had them all executed. But then what? The next lot wouldn't be any better, and their blood would not bring back all the soldiers she had lost, the provinces that now belonged to the Goyl, nor her dignity, which in the past months had been choked in the mud of four battlefields.

"Enough!"

One word, and the room where her great-grandfather used to sign death warrants fell silent. Power. Intoxicating. Like a fine wine.

How they bowed their vain heads. *Look at them, Therese. Wouldn't it be nice to have them all chopped off after all?*

The Empress adjusted the tiara of elven glass that her great-grandmother had worn before her, and waved one of the Dwarfs to her desk. Hers were the only Dwarfs in this land who still wore beards. Servants, bodyguards, confidants. Generations of service to her family, and still in the same livery they had worn for two hundred years. Lace collars over black velvet, and then those ridiculously wide breeches. Tasteless and completely unfashionable, but you couldn't argue with Dwarfs about tradition any more than you could argue with priests about religion.

"Write," she ordered.

The Dwarf climbed onto her chair. He had to kneel on the pale golden cushion. Auberon. Her favorite, and the smartest of them all. The hand that now reached for the quill was as small as a child's, but these hands would break iron chains as easily as her cooks' hands cracked an egg.

"We, Therese of Austry—" Her ancestors stared down at her disapprovingly. What did they know of Kings brought forth from the bowels of the earth, and a Fairy who turned human skin to stone to make it like the skin of her lover? "—herewith offer to Kami'en, King of the Goyl, our daughter Amalie's hand in marriage, to bring an end to the war and to bring peace to our two great nations."

How the silence erupted. As if her words had shattered the glass house in which they had all been sitting. But it wasn't she, it was the Goyl, who had struck the blow, and now she had to give him her daughter.

The Empress turned her back on them, silencing their angered voices. Only the rustle of her dress followed her as she stepped toward the high doors, which seemed to have been built not for humans but for the Giants, who, thanks to her great-grandfather's efforts, had been driven to extinction sixty years ago. *Power. Like wine when you have it. Like poison when you lose it.* Therese already felt it eating away at her.

Defeated.

14. Thorn Castle

"But he just won't wake up!" The voice sounded worried. And familiar. Fox.

"Don't worry. He's just sleeping." That voice he recognized as well. Clara.

Wake up, Jacob. Fingers stroked his searing shoulder. He opened his eyes and saw the silver moon drifting into a cloud, as if trying to hide from its red twin. It shone down into a dark

castle courtyard. High windows reflected the stars, though there was no light behind any of them. No lanterns shone above the doors or under the overgrown archways. No servant scuttled across the yard, which was thickly covered with wet leaves, as if it hadn't been raked in years.

"Finally! I thought you'd never wake up."

Jacob groaned as Fox nudged her nose into his shoulder.

"Fox! Be careful!"

Clara helped him sit up. She had put a fresh dressing on his shoulder, but it hurt more than ever. The bandits, the Goyl.... The pain brought it all back, but Jacob couldn't remember when he had lost consciousness.

Clara stood up. "That wound doesn't look good. I wish I had some pills from the hospital."

"It'll be fine," Jacob said. Fox anxiously nudged her head under his arm. "Where are we?" he asked her.

"At the only hiding place I could find. This is deserted—by the living, anyway." Fox dug aside the layers of leaves with her paw, revealing a shoe.

Jacob looked around. In many places the leaves lay suspiciously deep, as if covering outstretched bodies.

Where were they?

Jacob sought support from a wall to pull himself to his feet, and immediately he drew back his hands, cursing. The stones were covered in thorny vines. They were everywhere, as if the entire castle had grown a hide of thorns.

"Roses," he muttered, picking one of the rose hips that grew from the twisted branches. "I've been searching for this castle for years. Sleeping Beauty's bed. The Empress would pay a fortune for it."

Clara stared incredulously across the silent courtyard.

"It is said that anyone who sleeps in her bed will find true love. But it seems"—Jacob gazed at the dark windows—"the prince never showed up."

Or he had perished on the thorns like a skewered bird. A mummified hand stuck out from between the roses. Jacob pushed some leaves over it before Clara could see.

A mouse scampered across the courtyard, and Fox jumped after it, but she immediately stopped with a whimper.

"What is it?" Clara asked.

The vixen licked her side.

"Threefingers kicked me."

"Let me have a look." Clara leaned over her and carefully prodded her silky fur.

"Lose the fur, Fox!" Jacob said. "She knows more about humans than about foxes."

Fox hesitated, but then she obeyed. Clara stared at the girl who suddenly stood before her, in a dress that looked as if the red moon had woven it onto her body.

What kind of a world is this? her face asked as she turned to Jacob. *If fur turns to skin, or skin to stone, what remains?*

Fear. Bewilderment. And enchantment. All of that was in her eyes, and as she stepped toward Fox, she rubbed her own arms, as if she could already feel the fur on her skin as well.

"Where's Will?" Jacob asked.

Clara pointed at the tower next to the gate. "He's been up there for over an hour. He hasn't said a word yet," she added, "since he saw them."

They both knew whom she was talking about.

❦

Nowhere did the roses grow as densely as around the circular walls of the tower. Their blossoms were of such a dark red that the night tinged them almost black, and their scent hung heavily in the cold air, as if they did not feel the autumn.

Jacob already knew what he would find under the pointed roof before he started climbing the steep spiral stairs. He had to keep freeing his boots from the thorny tendrils, but finally he was standing in front of the room where, two hundred years earlier, a Fairy had delivered her birthday present.

The spinning wheel stood next to a narrow bed that had never been meant for a princess. The body that lay on it was covered with rose petals. The Fairy's curse had kept it from aging, but the princess's skin was like parchment and nearly as yellowed as the dress she'd been wearing for two centuries. The embroidered pearls still shimmered in brilliant white, but the lace at the hem had turned as brown as the petals that covered the silk.

Will was standing by the only window, as if the prince had finally arrived. Jacob's steps made him spin around. The stone now also stained his forehead, and the blue of his eyes was drowning in gold. The bandits had stolen what was most precious— time.

"No 'happily ever after' here," Will said, looking

over at the princess. "This was also the curse of a Fairy."

He leaned his back against the rough wall. "Are you feeling better?"

"Yes," Jacob answered, lying. "What about you?"

Will didn't answer right away. And when he did, his voice sounded as cool and smooth as his new skin.

"My face feels like polished stone. The night grows brighter with every passing day, and I could hear you long before you reached the stairs. I don't just feel it on my skin now." He hesitated, massaging his temples. "It's inside me as well."

He walked to the bed and stared at the mummified body. "I'd forgotten everything. You. Clara. Myself. All I knew was I wanted to ride to them."

Jacob searched for words, but he found none.

"Is that what's happening? Tell me the truth." Will looked at him. "I won't just look like them; I'll be like them. Won't I?"

Jacob had the lies ready on the tip of his tongue, all the "Nonsense, Will! Everything will be fine!" but they wouldn't pass his lips. His brother's look did not allow it.

"You want to know what they're like?" Will plucked a rose leaf from the princess's strawlike hair. "They're angry. Their rage bursts inside you like a flame. But they are also stone. They can feel it in the ground, breathing beneath them."

He examined the black nails on his hand.

"They are darkness," he said quietly. "And heat. And the red moon is their sun."

Jacob trembled as he heard the stone in his brother's voice.

Say something, Jacob. Anything. The dark chamber was so silent.

"You will not become like them," he finally said. "Because I am going to stop it."

"How?" There it was again, the glance that suddenly was so much older than he. "Is it true, what you told those bandits? You're taking me to another Fairy?"

"Yes."

"Is she as dangerous as the one who did this?" Will touched the brittle skin on the princess's face. "Look out the window. There are corpses hanging in the thorns. You think I want you to end like that for my sake?"

But Will's eyes belied his words. *Help me, Jacob,* they said. *Help me.*

Jacob pulled him away from the corpse.

"The Fairy I am taking you to is different," he said. *Is she, Jacob?* He heard a whisper inside him. But he ignored it.

He put all the hope he possessed into his voice. And all the confidence his brother wanted to hear: "She'll help us, Will, I promise!"

It still worked. Hope still spread over Will's face as easily as rage. Brothers. The elder and the younger. Unchanged.

15. SOFT FLESH

Threefingers with the butcher's face was the first to speak. Humans so liked to choose the wrong men as their leaders. Hentzau could see his cowardice as clearly as the watery blue of his eyes. But at least he had told them a few interesting details the moth had not shown Hentzau.

The Jade Goyl was not alone. He was with a

girl. Also—and this was even more important—he seemed to have a brother who had gotten it into his head to drive the jade from his body. If Threefingers was telling the truth, then the brother was planning to take the Jade Goyl to the Red Fairy. Not such a dumb idea. She despised her dark sister as much as the other Fairies did. Still, Hentzau was sure she wouldn't be able to break the curse. The Dark Fairy was so much more powerful than all the others.

No Goyl had ever seen the island that was home to the Fairies, let alone set foot on it. The Dark Fairy guarded the secrets of her sisters, even though they had cast her out, and everybody knew you could only reach their island if they wanted you to.

"How is he going to find her?"

"He didn't say!" Threefingers stammered.

Hentzau nodded to the only She-Goyl in his squad. He didn't enjoy striking human flesh. He could kill them, yes, but he avoided touching them. Nesser had no such qualms.

She kicked Threefingers in the face, and Hentzau gave her a look of warning. Her sister had been killed by humans, and so Nesser tended to overdo it. For a brief moment Nesser held his gaze, full of defiance, but then she lowered her head. Hatred had by now engulfed them all like slime.

"He didn't say," Threefingers stammered again. "I swear."

His flesh was as pale and as soft as a snail's. Hentzau turned away in disgust. He was certain they had told him all they knew, and it was because of them that the Jade Goyl had gotten away.

"Shoot them!" he ordered, and went outside.

The shots sounded strange in the silence, like something that didn't belong in this world. Guns, steam engines, trains; to Hentzau it still all felt unnatural. He was getting old—that was the trouble. The sunlight had clouded his eyes, and his hearing had been so damaged by all the battle noise that Nesser had to raise her voice whenever she addressed him. Kami'en acted as if he didn't notice. He knew Hentzau had aged in his service. But the Dark Fairy would make sure everybody else knew—as soon as she found out that a bunch of plunderers had made him lose the Jade Goyl.

Hentzau could still picture him standing there. The face, half Goyl, half human, the skin suffused with their holiest of stones. He wasn't the Jade Goyl. He couldn't be. He was as fake as one of those wooden fetishes, covered with gold leaf and sold to old women as solid gold. *"Behold, the Jade Goyl has come to make our King invincible. But don't cut too deep, or you will find human flesh."* Yes, that's what it was. Nothing but another attempt by the Fairy to make herself indispensable.

Hentzau squinted into the gathering night. Even the darkness turned to jade.

What if you're wrong, Hentzau? What if he is the real thing? What if your King's destiny depends on him? And he had let him get away.

When the scout finally returned, even Hentzau's dimmed eyes could see from his face that he had lost the trail. Once he would have killed the scout on the spot, but he'd learned to control the rage that lurked in all of them, although not half as well as his King.

That meant all he had to go on was what Threefingers had said about the Red Fairy. He would have to swallow his pride once more and send a messenger to the Dark Fairy to ask her for directions. The prospect pained him more than the cold night air.

"You will find me their tracks!" he barked at the scout. "As soon as it gets light. Three horses and a fox. Can't be that hard!"

He was just asking himself whom he should send to the Dark Fairy, when Nesser approached him. She was just thirteen years old. At that age Goyl were fully grown, but most of them didn't join the army until they were at least fourteen. Nesser was not very good with the saber, nor was she a particularly good shot, but her courage more than made up for those shortcomings. At her age, fear was an unfamiliar concept; you felt immortal, even without the blood of a Fairy coursing through your veins. Hentzau remembered the feeling all too well.

"Commander?"

He loved the reverence in her young voice. It was still the best antidote for the doubts the Dark Fairy had sown in him.

"What?"

"I know how to get to the Fairies. Not the island . . . but to the valley from where it can be reached."

"Is that so?" Hentzau did not show his relief. He was fond of the girl, and that made him even more strict with her. Like his own skin, Nesser's resembled brown jasper, though, as in all Goyl females, hers was suffused with amethyst.

"I was part of the escort the King sends with the Fairy when she goes traveling. I accompanied her on her last visit to her sisters. She left us to wait for her at the entrance to the valley, but..."

This was too good to be true. He would not have to beg for help. And nobody would need to know that the Jade Goyl had eluded him. Hentzau clenched his fist, but Nesser saw only his impassive face.

"All right," he said, his tone studiously uninterested. "Tell the scout you'll be leading the way from now on. But you'd better not get us lost."

"I won't, Commander!" Nesser's golden eyes glistened with confidence as she quickly walked away.

Hentzau just stared down the unpaved road in the direction the Jade Goyl had escaped. One of the looters had claimed that the brother was injured, and they would have to stop somewhere to sleep. Hentzau could go for days without sleep. He would be waiting for them.

16. NOT EVER

It was still dark when Jacob made them break camp. He desperately needed sleep, but not even Fox could convince him to rest longer, and Clara had to admit that she was glad to get away from all those sleeping dead.

It was a clear night. Black velvet, studded with stars. The trees and hills like silhouettes, and Will beside her but only seemingly close. So familiar and yet so strange.

Clara looked across at him, and he smiled back as his eyes met hers. But it was a mere shadow of the smile she knew. It had always been so easy to get a smile from him. Will gave love so freely. And it was so easy to love him back. Nothing had ever been as easy. She didn't want to lose him, but the world around her whispered, "He belongs to me." And they were riding deeper and deeper into it, as if they needed to find its heart to make it release his brother again.

Let him go!

Clara wanted to shout into the dismal face of this world.

Let him go!

But the world behind the mirror was also reaching out for her. She already felt its dark fingers on her own skin. "What do you want here?" the strange night whispered. "What skin shall I give you? Do you want fur? Do you want stone?"

"No," Clara whispered back. "I will find your heart, and you will give him back to me."

Yet Clara already felt her new skin growing. So soft. Far too soft. And she felt the dark fingers reaching for her own heart.

And she was so afraid.

17. A Guide to the Fairies

It was true what they said about the Fairies. Nobody came to them if they didn't want you to. That had also been true when Jacob had first searched for them three years ago, but even then there had been a way to find them.

You just had to bribe the right Dwarf.

There had always been those Dwarfs who claimed they traded with the Fairies and who

proudly displayed lilies on their family crests. Most of them, however, had just told Jacob dusty old tales about their ancestors before finally admitting that the last family member who had actually seen a Fairy had died more than a century ago. Finally, however, one of the Dwarfs at the imperial court had mentioned the name Evenaugh Valiant.

At that time, the Empress had offered a fortune in gold for a lily from the Fairy lake, for its scent was reputed to turn ugly girls into beautiful women. The prince consort had been declaring himself increasingly disappointed with the appearance of their only daughter. He had died shortly afterward in a hunting accident which, as sharp tongues had claimed, had been arranged by his own wife. But since the Empress had always valued her husband's taste more than the man himself, she had not withdrawn the reward for the lily, and so Jacob, who at that time was already working without Chanute, had set off to find Evenaugh Valiant.

Finding the Dwarf had not been hard, and for a sizable amount of gold, he actually led Jacob to the valley where the Fairies lived. But his guide had neglected to tell Jacob about the creatures that guarded the valley, and Jacob had nearly paid with his life for that little excursion. Valiant, however, sold the lily to the Empress, and it turned her daughter, Amalie, into an acclaimed beauty, and him into a purveyor to the court.

Jacob had imagined many times how he would settle his score with the Dwarf, but after he returned from the Fairies, he had lost his taste for revenge. He'd won the imperial gold through another assignment, and finally he had managed to push out of his mind any memory of Evenaugh Valiant or the island, where he had been so happy that he had nearly forgotten himself. *So what does that teach you, Jacob Reckless?* he wondered as the first Dwarf dwellings appeared among the fields and hedgerows. *That, on the whole, revenge is not such a great idea.* All the same, his heart clenched at the prospect of meeting the Dwarf again.

Not even the hood could conceal the stone on Will's face any longer, and Jacob decided to leave him and Clara behind with Fox while he rode into Terpevas (which, in the language of its inhabitants, means nothing else but "Dwarf City"). In a little wood, Fox found a cave that the local shepherds used as a shelter. Will followed his brother into its shade as if he couldn't wait to get out of the daylight. There was only a small patch of human skin left on his right cheek, and with every passing day Jacob found it harder to look at him. The eyes were the worst. Both were drowning in gold, and Jacob had to struggle ever harder against the fear that he might have already lost his race against time. Sometimes Will would return his glance as if he had already forgotten who he was, and Jacob thought he could see their shared past fading from his brother's eyes.

Clara had not followed them into the cave. When Jacob walked with Fox back to the horses, he saw her standing among the trees, still wearing men's clothes and looking so lost that for a moment Jacob mistook her for one of the orphan boys found everywhere in this world, waiting by the roadside, ready to do any kind of work. The autumn grass growing between the trees was the same color as her hair, and he could barely see the other world in her anymore. The memories of the streets and houses where they all had grown up, of the lights and the noise, and of the girl she had been there—all but faded, far away. The present swiftly became the past, and the future suddenly wore strange clothes.

"Will doesn't have much time left."

She didn't phrase it as a question. She faced things, even if they scared her. Jacob liked that about her.

"And you need a doctor," she said, seeing him flinch with pain as he swung himself onto the mare. All the flowers, leaves, and roots Fox had shown her had done nothing to check the infection in his shoulder. It was already making him feverish.

"She's right," said Fox. "Go to one of the Dwarf doctors. They're supposed to be even better than the Empress's personal physicians."

"Yes, if you're a Dwarf. Their only ambition with human patients is to make them pay and then send them to an early grave. Dwarfs don't think very highly of us," he added in response to Clara's puzzled look, "even those who serve the Empress. Nothing earns a Dwarf more prestige than having successfully fleeced a human."

"But you still know one you can trust?"

Fox uttered a scornful growl. She brushed around Clara's legs. Forging an alliance. "Trust? The Dwarf he's going to see is even less trustworthy than the others! Ask him where he got the scars on his back."

"That was a long time ago."

"And? Why should he have changed?" Anger had replaced the fear in Fox's voice.

Clara looked at Jacob with even more concern.

"Why don't you at least take Fox with you?"

For that, the vixen brushed around Clara's legs even more affectionately. She now always sought Clara's company, and for Clara she had even begun to shift into her human form more often.

Jacob turned the horse about.

"No. Fox stays here," he said.

Fox lowered her head and did not protest. She knew just as well as he did that neither Will nor Clara understood this world well enough to be left alone in it.

As Jacob reached the first bend in the road, he looked back and saw her, still sitting beside Clara, watching him ride away. His brother hadn't even asked him where he was going. Will was hiding from the sun.

18. WHISPERING STONE

Will heard the stone. He heard it as clearly as his own breathing. The sounds came from the cave walls, from the jagged ground beneath his feet, from the rocky ceiling above...vibrations to which his body responded as if it were made of them. He no longer had a name, only the new skin that cocooned him, cool and protective, and the new strength in his muscles, and the pain in his eyes when he looked at the sunlight.

He ran his hands over the rock, reading its age from its stony folds. They whispered to him about what was hidden beneath the innocuous gray surface: striped agate, pale white moonstone, golden citrine, black onyx. They showed him images: of underground cities, of petrified water, of dim light reflecting in windows of malachite. . . .

"Will?"

He turned around, and the rock fell silent.

A woman was standing in the cave's entrance, the sunlight clinging to her hair as if she were made of it.

Clara. Her face brought memories of another world, where stone had meant nothing more than walls and dead streets.

"Are you hungry? Fox caught a rabbit, and she showed me how to make a fire."

She stepped toward him and took his face between her hands, such soft hands, and so colorless against the green that was spreading through his skin. Her touch made him shudder, though Will tried to hide that from her. He loved her, didn't he?

If only her skin weren't so soft and pale.

"Can you hear anything?" he asked.

She looked at him, puzzled.

"Never mind," he said. And he kissed her, trying to forget how he suddenly longed to find amethyst in her skin. Her lips brought back more memories: of a house as high as a tower, of nights lit by artificial light and not by the gold in his eyes....

"I love you, Will." Clara whispered the words as if she wanted to banish the stone with them. But the stone whispered louder, and Will wanted to forget the name she'd called him.

I love you, too. He wanted to say it, because he knew he'd said it so many times before. But he was no longer sure what it meant or whether it could be felt by a heart of stone.

"It will be okay," she whispered. She stroked his face, as if trying to feel his old flesh under the new skin. "Jacob will be back soon."

Jacob. Another name. Pain clung to it, and he remembered how all too often he had called that name without receiving an answer. Empty rooms. Empty days.

Jacob. Clara. Will.

He wanted to forget them all.

He pushed away the soft hands.

"Don't," he said. "Don't touch me."

How she looked at him. Pain. Love. Blame. He'd seen it all before, on another face: his mother's. Too much pain. Too much love. He didn't want all that anymore. He wanted the stone, cool and firm, so different from all the softness, the yielding, the vulnerability, and the lachrymose flesh.

He turned his back to her. "Go away," he said. "Just leave already."

And he listened to the rock again, let it paint pictures and turn to stone what was soft in him.

19. Valiant

Terpevas was the largest city of the Dwarfs. It was more than twelve hundred years old, if their records were to be believed. And yet the large hoardings on the city walls, advertising anything from beer and eyeglasses to patented gas lamps, made it clear to any visitor that no one took the modern times more seriously than the Dwarfs. They were restless, traditional, grouchy,

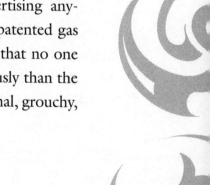

and inventive, and their trading posts could be found in every corner of this world, though the Dwarfs themselves barely reached the hips of most of their customers. In addition, their reputation as spies was unrivaled.

The traffic in front of the gates of Terpevas was nearly as congested as it was on the other side of the mirror, though here the noise came from carts, carriages, and horses vying for space on the gray cobblestones. The Dwarfs' customers came from everywhere, and the war had only increased business. They had been trading with the Goyl for a long time, and the Stone King had made many of them his chief purveyors. Evenaugh Valiant, the Dwarf whom Jacob had come to see, had also been trading with the Goyl for years, staying true to his motto of always getting on the winning side in time.

Let's just hope the devious little bastard is still alive! Jacob thought to himself as he steered his mare past coaches and chaises and toward the city's southern gate. After all, it was perfectly possible that by now some cheated customer had bludgeoned Valiant to death.

It would have taken three Dwarfs standing on top of one another to look into the eyes of one of the sentries by the gate. Only those men who could prove their direct descent from the extinct race of the Giants were hired to guard Terpevas's gates. The Giantlings, as they were referred to, were highly sought after as guards and mercenaries, even though they were generally not thought to be very bright. The Dwarfs paid them so well that they even squeezed themselves into the old-fashioned uniforms used by their employers' army. Not even the imperial cavalry wore helmets plumed with swan feathers anymore, but the Dwarfs liked to decorate the modern era with the reassuring uniforms of more traditional times.

As Jacob rode past the Giantlings, he fell in behind two Goyl. One of them had a skin of moonstone; the other's was onyx. Their attire was not any different from that of the human factory owners whose carriage the Giantlings waved through behind them— though their tailcoats revealed the distinct bulges of pistol handles. Their wide lapels were embroidered with jade and moonstone, and the dark glasses with which they shielded their sensitive eyes were made of onyx, cut thinner than any human stonecutter could have ever achieved.

The two Goyl ignored the fear and disgust their presence clearly elicited in all the human visitors to the Dwarf city. Their faces said it quite clearly: This world belonged to them now. Their King had plucked it like a ripe fruit, and all those who, until a few years ago, had hunted them like animals were now burying their soldiers in mass graves and begging for peace.

The onyx-skinned Goyl removed his glasses, and his gold-drenched glance so resembled Will's that Jacob reined in his horse and stared after him until the angry shouts of a Dwarf woman with two tiny children whose path he was blocking brought him back to his senses.

Dwarf city. Shrunken world.

Jacob left the mare in one of the stables by the city wall. Terpevas's main roads were as wide as the streets of the humans, but beyond those there was no denying that the city's inhabitants were barely larger than a six-year-old child, and some of the alleyways were so narrow that Jacob could barely pass through them even on foot. All the cities of the Mirrorworld were spreading like fungi, and Terpevas was no exception. Smoke from countless coal furnaces blackened the windows and the walls, and the cold autumn air certainly did not smell of damp leaves, even though the Dwarfs' sewer system was vastly superior to that of the Empress. With every year Jacob spent in it, the world behind the mirror seemed more desperate to catch up with its sister on the other side.

Jacob could barely decipher the street signs, for he had acquired only a very scant knowledge of the Dwarf alphabet, and soon enough he was hopelessly lost. After the third time Jacob hit his head on the same barber's sign, he finally stopped a messenger boy and asked him for directions to the house of Evenaugh Valiant, Importer and Exporter of Rare Objects of Any Kind. The boy barely reached his knee, but his demeanor immediately became more friendly as Jacob counted two copper coins into his tiny hand. His diminutive guide darted through the crowded alleys so quickly that Jacob had trouble keeping up with him, but finally they stopped in front of the same entrance Jacob had squeezed himself through three years earlier.

Valiant's name was etched in golden letters on the frosted glass, and just as before Jacob had to duck his head to fit through the doorframe. Valiant's reception room was just tall enough for his human clients to be able to stand upright in it. The walls were decorated with photographs of his most influential customers. Even in the Mirrorworld people no longer had themselves painted but photographed, and nothing attested to Valiant's business acumen better than the fact that the portrait of the Empress was hanging right next to that of a Goyl officer. The frames were made of moon-silver, and the chandelier hanging from the ceiling was inlaid with the glass hairs of a Djinn, which must have cost the Dwarf a fortune. Everything indicated that business was good. There were two secretaries instead of the one grumpy Dwarf woman who had greeted Jacob on his first visit.

The smaller of the two didn't even lift his head as Jacob stood in front of his barely knee-high desk. The other one eyed him with the customary disdain Dwarfs displayed toward all humans, including those they were doing business with.

Jacob gave him his friendliest smile.

"I take it Mr. Valiant still does business with the Fairies?"

"Indeed. But we don't have any moth cocoons in stock at the moment." The secretary's voice, like that of most Dwarfs, was surprisingly deep. "Try us again in three months."

With that, he turned his attention back to his papers, but his head shot up again as Jacob cocked his pistol with a soft click.

"I'm not here for moth cocoons. Would you both

be kind enough to step into that wardrobe over there?"

The strength of Dwarfs was legendary, but these two were rather scrawny specimens, and Valiant obviously didn't pay them enough to risk being shot by some passing human. They let themselves be locked up in the wardrobe without any resistance. It looked solid enough to ensure that they couldn't call the Dwarf police while Jacob had a chat with their employer.

The crest that was proudly displayed on Valiant's office door showed, above the Fairy lily, the heraldic animal of the Valiants, the badger, sitting on a mound of gold coins.

The door on which it hung was made of rosewood, a material known not only for its high price but also for its superior soundproofing qualities, which meant that Valiant hadn't noticed any of what had been going on in his front office.

He was sitting behind a human-sized desk, the legs of which had been shortened. His eyes were closed, and he was puffing on a cigar that would have looked huge even in the mouth of a Giantling. Evenaugh Valiant had shaved his beard, as was now the fashion among Dwarfs. The eyebrows, usually as bushy as those of all his race, had been carefully trimmed, and his bespoke suit was made of velvet, a material rich Dwarfs coveted more than any other. Jacob would have loved to pluck him out of his wolf-leather chair and toss him through the window behind him, but the memory of Will's petrified face held him back.

"I asked not to be disturbed, Banster." The Dwarf sighed without opening his eyes. "Don't tell me it's about that stuffed Waterman again."

He'd grown fat. And older. The curly red hair was already turning gray, early for a Dwarf. Most of them lived to be at least a hundred, and Valiant was barely sixty, unless he'd also lied about his age.

"No, a stuffed Waterman isn't quite what I'm after," Jacob said, pointing his pistol at the curly head. "But three years ago, I paid for services I never received."

Valiant nearly choked on his cigar. He looked at Jacob as dumbfoundedly as one would at a visitor one had left to the mercy of a stampeding herd of Unicorns.

"Jacob Reckless!" he said, panting.

"Well, I never! You actually remember my name."

The Dwarf dropped his cigar, and his hand reached under the desk, but he quickly pulled his stubby fingers back as Jacob slit his tailored sleeve with the saber.

"Careful, now!" Jacob said. "You don't need both your arms to take me to the Fairies. And you don't need your ears or your nose, either. Hands behind your head. Now!"

Valiant obeyed. As he raised his hands, his mouth twisted into far too broad a smile.

"Jacob!" he purred. "What is this? Of course I knew you weren't dead. After all, everybody's heard your story. Jacob Reckless, the fortunate mortal who was kept by the Red Fairy for a year. Every male creature in the land, be he Dwarf, human, or Goyl, is green with envy at the mere thought of it. Go on: Admit it! Whom do you have to thank for that? Evenaugh Valiant. Had I warned you about the Unicorns, you would've been turned into a thistle or a fish, like any other uninvited visitor. But not even the Red Fairy can resist a man who's lying, helpless, in his own blood."

Jacob had to admire the Dwarf's brazen logic.

"Tell me!" Valiant whispered across his oversize desk without even a hint of remorse. "How was she? And how did you manage to get away?"

Jacob grabbed the Dwarf by his bespoke lapels and pulled him out from behind his desk. "This is my onetime offer: I won't shoot you, and in return you'll take me to their valley once again, but this time you show me how to get past the Unicorns."

"What?" Valiant tried to wriggle free, but Jacob's pistol quickly changed his mind. "It's a two-day ride, at least!" he whined. "I can't just leave my business!"

Jacob simply shoved him toward the door.

The two secretaries were whispering in the wardrobe. Valiant glared in their direction as he plucked his hat from the coatrack by the door.

"My prices have increased considerably in the past three years," he said.

"I'll let you live," Jacob replied. "That's more of a raise than you deserve."

Valiant gave him a pitying smile as he adjusted his hat in the glass of his front door. Like most Dwarfs, he was partial to black top hats, which added a fair number of inches to his stature.

"You seem to be desperate to get back to your old flame," he purred, "and the price always rises with the desperation of the customer."

In reply, Jacob tapped the muzzle of his gun against the Dwarf's hat. "Trust me," he said, "this customer is desperate enough to shoot you at a moment's notice."

20. Too Much

Fox smelled golden revulsion, petrified loathing, frozen love. The entrance of the cave
exhaled it all, and her fur bristled when she
found Clara's tracks on the grass in front of it.
She had stumbled more than walked, and her
tracks led toward the trees growing behind the
cave. Fox had heard Jacob warn Clara about
those trees, but she'd rushed toward them as if

their ominous shadows were exactly what she was looking for.

Clara's scent was the same one Fox smelled on herself whenever she lost her fur. Girl. Woman. So much more vulnerable. Strong and yet weak. A heart that knew no armor. The scent told Fox about all the things she feared and from which the fur protected her. Clara's hasty steps wrote them onto the dark soil, and Fox didn't need her nose to know why Clara was running. She herself had tried to run from pain before.

The hazel bushes and wild apple trees were harmless, but between them grew trunks with bark as spiny as the shell of a chestnut. Bird-trees. Under their branches the sunlight dissolved into a gloomy brown, and Clara had stumbled right into the wooden claws of one of them. She screamed for Jacob, but he was far away. The tree curled its roots around her arms and ankles, and its feathery servants already descended on her body, their plumage as white as virgin snow, birds with sharp beaks and eyes like red berries.

Fox jumped among them, her teeth bared, deaf to their angry cries. She snapped one of the birds in midjump, before it could escape to the safety of the branches. She felt its heart racing between her jaws, but she did not bite; she just held on firmly, very firmly, until the tree let go of Clara with an angry groan.

The roots slid off Clara like snakes, and as she struggled back to her feet, they were already slipping beneath the autumn-brown leaves, where they would be in wait for their next victim. The other birds chattered angrily from the branches, ghostly white creatures among the yellowing foliage. But Fox held on to her quarry until Clara staggered to her side.

Her face was as white as the feathers that stuck to her dress. Fox could smell not only the mortal fear on her body but also the pain in her heart, raw, like a fresh wound.

They barely spoke a word on their way back to the cave. At one point Clara stopped, as if she could not go on, but then she did, wordlessly. When they reached the cave, she looked at the dark entrance as if she hoped to see Will there, but then she just crouched down in the grass next to the horses, with her back to the cave. She was unharmed, apart from a few small grazes on her throat and ankles, but Fox saw how ashamed she was, of her aching heart and for having run away.

Fox didn't want her to leave. She shifted her shape

and put her arms around Clara, who pressed her face against the furry dress that so much resembled the vixen's coat.

"He doesn't love me anymore."

"He doesn't love anybody anymore," Fox whispered back. "He's forgetting who he is."

She knew how it felt. Another skin, another person. But the fur she had grown was soft and warm. The stone was so hard and cold.

Clara looked toward the cave. Fox picked a feather from her hair.

"Don't leave!" Fox whispered to her. "Jacob will help him. You'll see."

If only he were back already.

21. His Brother's Keeper

As Jacob rode toward the cave, Fox came running to him. Will and Clara were nowhere to be seen.

"Will you look at that! That mangy vixen still following you around?" Valiant jeered as Jacob lifted him from the horse. Jacob had tied him with a silver chain, the only metal that Dwarfs could not snap like thread.

Jacob would not have been surprised if Fox

had replied to Valiant's remark with a bite, but she seemed not to have even noticed the Dwarf. Something had happened. Her fur was standing on end, and she had some white feathers stuck to her back.

"You have to talk to your brother," she said while Jacob tied the Dwarf to a nearby tree.

"What happened?" Jacob cast a worried glance at the cave where Will was hiding, but Fox pointed toward the horses. Clara was there, sleeping in the shade of a beech. Her shirt was torn, and Jacob could see blood on her throat.

"They had a fight," Fox said. "He no longer knows what he's doing."

The stone is faster than you, Jacob.

⚜

Jacob found Will in the darkest corner of the cave. He was sitting on the floor, his back against the rock.

The roles have been switched, Jacob. It had always been he who, after doing some mischief, had sat in the dark—in his bedroom, in the laundry room, in his father's study. *"Jacob? Where are you? What have you done now?"* Always Jacob, but not Will. Never Will.

His brother's eyes gleamed in the dark like gold coins.

"What did you say to Clara?"

Will looked at his fingers and clenched them into a fist.

"I can't remember."

"Don't give me that!"

Will had never been a good liar.

"You're the one who wanted to bring her along. Or can't you remember that, either?"

Jacob, stop it. But his shoulder was throbbing with pain, and he was sick and tired of having to look after his brother.

"Fight it!" he yelled at Will. "You can't always count on me to do it all for you."

Will slowly got to his feet. His movements had become more sinewy, and the times when he had barely reached up to Jacob's shoulders had long passed.

"Count on you?" he said. "I quit doing that when I was five. Our mother took a little longer, though. And it was I who got to listen to her crying herself to sleep at night for years."

Brothers.

It was as if they were back in the apartment, in the wide hallway with all the empty rooms and the dark spot on the wallpaper where their father's photograph had once hung.

"Since when does it make any sense to trust some-one who is never there?"

Will's voice dispensed his splinters casually, but they still stung.

"You have a lot in common with him, not just your looks."

He scrutinized Jacob as if he were comparing his brother's face with their father's.

"Don't you worry. I am fighting it," he said. "After all, it's my skin, not yours. And I'm still here, right? Doing what you tell me to do. Riding behind you. Sucking it up."

Valiant's voice could be heard outside. He was trying to convince Fox to free him from his silver shackles.

Will nodded toward the exit. "Is that the guide you were talking about?"

"Yes." Jacob forced himself to look at this stranger with his brother's features.

Will walked toward the opening, shielding his eyes with his hand as the sunlight found his face. "I am sorry for what I said to Clara," he said. "I'll talk to her."

Then he stepped outside. And Jacob stood in the darkness, still feeling the splinters—as if Will had smashed the mirror.

22. Dreams

It was night, but the Dark Fairy did not sleep. The night was too beautiful to sleep it away. But she still saw the Man-Goyl anyway. By now she dreamed of him whether she was asleep or not. Her curse had already turned most of his skin to jade. Jade. Green. Like life itself. Petrified abundance. Heart-stone, sown by the heartless. He would be so much more beautiful

once the jade had replaced all his human skin, and once he fulfilled the promise of his new flesh. The future, as decided by the past, all those things hidden in the folds of time. They could only be known in dreams, which revealed so much more to her than to men or Goyl, perhaps because time meant so little when you were immortal.

She should have stayed in the castle with the bricked-up windows and waited there for news from Hentzau, but Kami'en wanted to get back to the mountains where he was born and return to his fortress under the earth. He longed for the deep as she longed for the night sky and for white lilies floating on water—although she still tried to convince herself that love alone could feed her soul.

All she saw in the train window was her own reflection, a pale phantom on a pane of glass, behind which the world slipped past far too quickly. Kami'en knew that she disliked trains almost as much as she disliked the depths of the earth, so he'd had the walls of her carriage decorated with intarsia: ruby blossoms and malachite leaves, a sky of lapis lazuli, hills of jade, and, inlaid with moonstone, the shimmering surface of a lake. That was love, wasn't it?

The stone images were beautiful, very beautiful,

and whenever she no longer could bear seeing the hills and fields rush by as if they were dissolving into the fabric of time, she would run her fingers over the inlaid blossoms. And yet the noise of the train still hurt her ears, and all the metal around her made her Fairy skin crawl.

Yes. He loved her. But he was still going to marry the dollface, the human princess with the blank eyes and the beauty she owed to the lilies of the Fairies. Amalie. Her name sounded as bland as her face looked. How she would have loved to kill her. A poisoned comb, a dress that would eat into her flesh while she twirled in it in front of her golden mirrors. How she would scream and tear at her skin, which was so much softer than that of her bridegroom.

The Fairy pressed her forehead against the cool glass. She couldn't understand where all that jealousy was coming from. After all, it wasn't the first time Kami'en had taken himself another woman. No Goyl loved only once. Nobody loved only once...Fairies least of all.

The Dark Fairy knew all the stories about her kind: that those who loved one of them invariably fell into madness; that they had no hearts, just as they had neither fathers nor mothers. At least that part was true. She pressed her hand against her chest. No heart. So where did the love she felt come from?

Outside, the stars were floating like blossoms on the inky waters of a river. The Goyl feared water, even though it had created their caves, and the sound of its dripping was as natural a part of their cities as the sound of the wind above the ground. They feared water so much that the sea had restricted Kami'en's conquests, making him dream of the power of flight. But she couldn't give him wings, any more than she could give him children. She was born of the water he feared so much, and all the words that meant so much to them—sister, brother, daughter, son—meant nothing to her.

The dollface couldn't give him children, either, unless he wanted to sire one of those crippled monsters some human women had borne his soldiers. *"How often do I have to tell you? I couldn't care less about her, but I need this peace."* He actually believed every one of his words, but she knew him better than that. He did want peace, but even more than that he yearned to caress human skin and to make one of them his wife. His fascination with all things human had begun to concern her as much as it did his people.

Where did the love come from? What was it made of? Stone, like him? Water, like her?

When she had first set out to find him, it had just been a game. A game with the toy her dreams had shown her. The Goyl who was smashing the world to pieces, who disregarded its rules, just as she did. The Fairies played with this world; the last one to have done so now wore a skin of bark. And yet she had still dispatched her moths to find Kami'en. The tent in which she first met him had smelled of blood, of the death she did not understand, and still she had thought of it all as a game. She had promised him the world. His flesh in the flesh of his enemies. And much too late had she realized what he had sown in her. Love. Worst of all poisons.

"You should wear human dresses more often."

Eyes of gold. Lips of fire. He didn't look tired, even though he had barely slept in days.

The Fairy's dress rustled as she turned. Human women dressed like flowers, layers of petals around a mortal, rotting core. She had had the dress made in the likeness of one of the paintings that hung in the dead general's castle. Kami'en had gazed at it often, as if it showed a world he longed for. The fabric would have made ten dresses, but she loved the rustling of the silk and its cool smoothness on her skin.

"No news from Hentzau?"

As if she didn't know the answer. Why had her moths still not found the one she was looking for? She could see him so clearly—as if she only had to reach out to feel his jade skin at her fingertips.

"Hentzau will find him, if he exists." Kami'en stood behind her. He doubted her dreams but never his jasper shadow.

Hentzau. Someone else she would have loved to kill. But Kami'en would forgive his death even less than that of his future bride. He had killed his own brothers, as the Goyl often did, but Hentzau was closer to him than a brother. Maybe even closer than she was.

Their reflections in the train window melted into one. Her breath still quickened whenever he stood near her. Where does love come from?

"Forget the Jade Goyl. Forget your dreams," he whispered, undoing her hair. "I will give you new dreams. Just tell me what you want."

She'd never told Kami'en that she had also found him first in her dreams. He wouldn't have liked it. Neither Goyl nor men lived long enough to understand that yesterday was born of tomorrow, just as tomorrow was born of yesterday.

23. TRAPPED

When Jacob rode into the gorge through which he had once before entered the valley of the Fairies, he felt as if he were riding into his own past. Nothing seemed to have changed in three years: the creek running along the bottom, the spruces clawing into the slopes, the silence between the rocks.... Only his shoulder reminded him of how much had happened

since. It still felt as if the Tailor was stitching seams through his skin.

Valiant was sitting in front of him. He kept turning, clearly delighted at how awful Jacob was feeling.

"Oh, you really look terrible, Reckless!" he observed for the umpteenth time, with undisguised glee. "That poor girl is staring at you again. She's probably terrified you'll fall off your horse before her boyfriend can get his skin back. Don't you worry, though. After you're dead and your brother has turned into a Goyl, I'll console her. I'm quite partial to human women."

It had been like that ever since they set out, but Jacob was too dazed by the fever to reply. Even the words Will had said to him in the cave no longer penetrated his agony, and by now he longed for the healing air of the Fairy's realm as much for his own sake as for his brother's.

Not far now, Jacob. You just have to get through the gorge, and then you're in their valley.

Clara was riding right behind him. Every now and then, Will rode up next to her, as if trying to make her forget what had happened in the cave. Love and fear were battling each other on her face. But she rode on. Like him. Like Will.

And the Dwarf could still betray them all.

The sun was already standing quite low, and the shadows between the rocks were growing. The foaming creek along which they rode was so dark it looked like it was carrying the night into the gorge, and they had not gotten very far when Will suddenly reined in his horse.

"What is it?" Valiant asked anxiously.

"There are Goyl here." There was not a trace of doubt in Will's voice.

"Goyl?" Valiant cast a malicious glance at Jacob. "Excellent. I get on great with the Goyl."

Jacob put his hand over the Dwarf's mouth. He slackened the mare's reins and listened, but the rush of the water drowned out all other sounds. "Act as if we're watering the horses," he whispered to Clara and Will.

"I smell them, too!" Fox hissed. "Dead ahead."

"But why are they hiding?" Will shuddered, like an animal catching the scent of its pride.

Valiant looked at him as if he saw him for the first time. Then he spun around so abruptly that he nearly fell off the horse.

"You cunning dog!" he hissed at Jacob. "What's the color of the stone in his skin? Green, right?"

"So what?"

"So what? Don't take me for a fool! It's jade. The Goyl are offering two pounds of red moonstone for him. Your brother, indeed! Don't make me laugh!" The Dwarf gave him a conspiratorial wink. "You found him—just like you found the glass slipper and the wishing table. But why are you taking him to the Fairies?"

Jade.

Jacob stared at Will's pale green skin. He had, of course, heard the stories. The Goyl King and his invincible bodyguard. Chanute had once fantasized about finding him and selling him to the Empress. But they couldn't seriously think his brother was the Jade Goyl.

He could see the mist-shrouded valley at the end of the gorge. So close.

"Let's take him to one of their fortresses and split the reward!" Valiant hissed again. "If they capture him here, they won't give us anything for him."

But Jacob ignored him.

He saw Will shudder.

"Is there another way into the valley?" Jacob asked the Dwarf.

"Sure," Valiant replied with a smirk, "if you think

your so-called brother has time to go the long way around...not to mention yourself."

Will looked around like a caged animal.

Clara steered her horse next to Jacob's. "Get him away from here!" she whispered. "Please!"

But then what?

A few yards away, a group of pine trees grew in front of the rocks. It was so dark under their branches that even as close as this, Jacob couldn't see beneath them.

Jacob leaned over to Will and reached for his arm.

"Follow me to those pines," he whispered to him. "Dismount when I do."

It was time to play some hide-and-seek and fancy-dress.

Will hesitated, but then he picked up his reins and rode after Jacob. The shade under the pines was as black as soot—darkness that, with luck, would conceal them even from Goyl eyes.

"Remember how we fought when we were kids?" Jacob whispered to Will before he dismounted.

"You always let me win."

"That's exactly what we'll do now."

Fox ran to Jacob's side.

"What are you doing?"

"No matter what happens," he whispered to her, "I want you to stay with Will. Promise me. If you don't, we'll all die."

Will climbed out of the saddle.

"I want you to fight back, Will, and it has to look real," Jacob whispered. "We need to end up under those trees."

Then, without warning, he punched his brother in the face.

Immediately the gold in Will's eyes flared up.

He hit back so hard that Jacob fell to his knees. Skin of stone, and a rage that he had never seen before on his brother's face.

Maybe not such a good plan after all, Jacob.

24. The Hunters

Hentzau had reached the ravine at daybreak. The Unicorns grazing in the misty valley beyond had left him with little doubt that Nesser had led them to the right place. However, as the sun sank ever lower, he began to ask himself whether the Jade Goyl had been shot by his brother after all. But then Nesser pointed silently toward the end of the gorge.

They had a girl and a fox with them, just as Threefingers had said. And they had caught themselves a Dwarf. Not dumb. Not even Nesser knew how to get past the Unicorns, but Hentzau had heard the rumors that some Dwarfs knew the secret. Be that as it may, Hentzau had no ambition to be the first Goyl to see the Fairies' island. He would rather have ridden through a dozen Hungry Forests or slept with the blind snakes in the depths of the earth. No. He would get the Jade Goyl before he could hide behind the Unicorns.

"Commander! They're fighting each other." Nesser sounded surprised.

What did she expect? The rage came with the stone skin, just like the gold in the eyes, and who would feel the brunt of it first? The brother, of course. *Yes! Kill him!* Hentzau thought, watching the Jade Goyl through his spyglass. *Maybe there have been times when you wanted to do just that, but he was always the older, the stronger. You'll see: The rage of the Goyl more than makes up for that.*

The older brother fought quite well, but he didn't stand a chance.

There. He fell to his knees. The girl ran to the Jade Goyl and pulled him away, but he shook her off, and as his brother struggled back to his feet, he kicked him in the chest so hard that he staggered back under the trees. The blackness beneath the branches swallowed them both, and Hentzau was just about to give the order to ride down, when the Jade Goyl reappeared from under the leaves.

He was already recoiling from the glare of the sun, pulling his hood down over his face as he headed toward his horse. The fight had made his step a little unsteady, but he would soon feel how much quicker his new flesh healed.

"Mount up!" Hentzau whispered to Nesser. "Let's catch ourselves a fairy tale!"

25. THE BAIT

Rocks. Shrubs. Where could they be hiding? *How would you know, Jacob? You're not a Goyl. Maybe you should have asked your brother.*

Jacob pulled the hood closer around his face and forced the horse into a slow gait. How could the Goyl have known they'd be coming through this gorge? *Not now, Jacob.*

He couldn't tell which hurt more, the shoulder

or his face. Human flesh was so soft compared to jade knuckles. For a few terrible moments, he had really thought Will would beat him to death. He still wasn't sure how much of the rage he'd felt in those blows was that of the Goyl and how much was his brother's.

Water sprayed on his feverish skin as he urged Will's horse through the creek. The hoofbeats echoed through the narrow gorge, and Jacob was beginning to wonder whether Will hadn't just sensed the Goyl in his own flesh, when suddenly there was movement on the slope to his left.

Now. He slackened the reins. Will's bay gelding was not as fast as the mare but very hardy, and Jacob was an excellent rider.

They of course tried to cut him off, but their horses shied on the loose rubble. Just as he had hoped. The gelding dashed past them, galloping into the misty valley. Immediately Jacob was assaulted by memories that seemed to have been lying in wait for him among these mountains. Happiness and love. Fear and death.

The Unicorns lifted their heads. Of course they weren't white. Why were things in his world always whitewashed? Their hides were brown and gray, mottled black, and pale yellow like the autumn sun drifting through the damp fog above. They were watching him, but so far none of them looked ready to attack.

Jacob looked around at his pursuers.

There were five of them. He immediately recognized the officer. It was the same one who had led the Goyl at the farm. His jasper-brown skin was cracked at the forehead, as if someone had tried to split it open, and one of his golden eyes was as cloudy as watery milk. So they really were following him.

Jacob leaned down over the neck of the horse. The gelding's hooves sank deep into the damp grass, but fortunately he hardly slowed down.

Ride, Jacob. Draw them away, before your brother gets it into his head to join them.

The Goyl were coming closer, but they didn't shoot. Of course not. If they believed Will was the Jade Goyl, then they'd want him alive.

One of the Unicorns whinnied. Jacob shot a look at the herd. *Stay where you are.*

Another glance over his shoulder. The Goyl had split up. They were trying to encircle him. The pain from the wound made his eyes water, and for a moment Jacob thought he was falling back through time, and he saw himself lying on the grass again with a hole in his back.

Faster. He had to be faster. But the gelding was already panting heavily, and sadly the Goyl no longer rode those half-blind horses they bred under the earth. One of them was getting very close. The officer. Jacob averted his face, but the hood slipped off his head just as he tried to reach for it.

The surprise on the jasper face quickly turned into rage, the same rage Jacob had already seen in his brother.

The game was up.

Where was Will? Jacob glanced desperately behind him. The Goyl officer was looking in the same direction.

His brother was galloping straight at the Unicorns, with the Dwarf perched in front of him. He was riding Clara's horse and had given her the mare. The grass beside her rippled as if the wind were blowing over it. Fox. Nearly as fast on her paws as the horses.

Jacob drew the pistol, but his left hand no longer obeyed him, and he was a much worse shot with his right. Still, he managed to shoot two Goyl out of their saddles as they turned and headed toward Will. The Milk-Eye leveled his gun at him, his jasper face stiff with rage. The anger had made him forget which brother he was supposed to hunt, but his horse stumbled in the high grass, and his bullet missed its mark.

Faster, Jacob. He barely managed to stay in the saddle. Will had nearly reached the Unicorns. Jacob prayed the Dwarf had told them the truth this time. *Ride!* he thought desperately, but Will suddenly slowed down. He brought his horse to a halt, and Jacob knew it wasn't out of concern for him. Will turned in the saddle and stared at the Goyl, just as he had done at the farm.

Milk-Eye had meanwhile remembered whom he was charged to capture. Jacob took aim, but his shot just grazed the jasper skin. Damned right hand!

And Will turned his horse.

Jacob screamed his name.

One of the Goyl had nearly reached Will. It was a female, amethyst on brown jasper. She drew her saber as Clara steered her horse protectively in front of Will's. But Jacob's bullet was faster. The Milk-Eye uttered a hoarse howl as the She-Goyl fell, and drove his horse even harder toward Will. Just a few more yards. The Dwarf was staring, wide-eyed, toward the Goyl. But Clara had gotten hold of Will's reins, and the horse she had ridden so many times yielded as she pulled it toward the Unicorns.

The herd had watched the hunt as indifferently as humans would watch a group of squabbling sparrows.

Jacob forgot to breathe as Clara rode toward them, but this time the Dwarf really had told the truth. The Unicorns let Will and Clara pass.

It was only when the Goyl rode toward them that they attacked.

The valley filled with shrill whinnies, beating hooves, and rearing bodies. Jacob heard shots. *Forget the Goyl, Jacob. Follow your brother!*

His heart pounding in his throat, he rode toward the agitated herd. He imagined he could once more feel the Unicorn horns tearing into his back, warm blood running down his skin. *Not this time, Jacob. Do as the Dwarf told you. "It's easy. Close your eyes and keep them shut, or they will skewer you."*

A horn brushed his thigh. Nostrils snorted in his ear. The cold air carried the scent of horse and deer. *Keep your eyes closed, Jacob.* The sea of shaggy bodies seemed endless. His left arm felt dead, and his right hand clutched the neck of the gelding. Then, suddenly, he no longer heard snorting but the wind in a thousand leaves, the lapping of water, and the rustling of reeds.

He opened his eyes, and it was just as it had been back then.

Everything had vanished. The Goyl, the Unicorns,

the misty valley. Instead, a lake glistened under the evening sky. On it floated the lilies for which he had ventured here three years earlier. The leaves on the willows by the shore were as fresh and green as newly emerged shoots. And in the distance, drifting on the waves, lay the island from which there was no return. *Except for you, Jacob.*

The warm air caressed his skin, and the pain in his shoulder ebbed away like the water on the reed-lined shore.

He slid off the exhausted gelding.

Clara and Fox rushed toward him. Will, however, was standing by the shore, staring across at the island. He seemed unhurt, but when he turned to face Jacob, his eyes were still on fire, and the jade was speckled with just a few last remnants of his human skin.

"Here we are. Happy?" Valiant stood between the willows. He was plucking Unicorn hairs from his sleeve.

"Who took off your chain?" Jacob tried to grab the Dwarf, but Valiant dodged him nimbly.

"Luckily a female heart is much more compassionate than the piece of rock that's rumbling around in your chest," he purred while Clara sheepishly returned Jacob's glance. "And? What are you getting all huffy about? We're even! Except for the fact that the Unicorns trampled my hat!" Valiant accusingly patted his graying curls. "You could at least pay for that!"

"Us? Even? Shall I show you the scars on my back?" Jacob rubbed his shoulder. It felt as if he had never fought against the Tailor. "Just get out of here," he said to the Dwarf. "Before I shoot you after all."

"Really?" Valiant cast a contemptuous look at the island drifting in the distance. "I'm quite sure I'll live to see your name chiseled onto a gravestone long before mine. M'lady," he said, turning to Clara, "you should come with me. This will not end well. Have you ever heard of Snow-White, the human girl who lived with some Dwarf brothers before falling for one of the Empress's ancestors? She ended up very miserable and finally ran away from him—with a Dwarf!"

"Really?" murmured Clara, but she didn't seem to have been listening. She stepped toward the shore of the blossom-covered lake as if she had forgotten everything around her, even Will, who was standing just a few yards away. Bluebells grew between the willows, their petals mirroring the dark blue of the evening sky. She picked one, and it chimed softly, wiping all the fear and sadness from her face. Valiant uttered an exasperated groan.

"Fairy magic!" he muttered scornfully. "I think I'd better take my leave."

"Wait!" said Jacob. "There used to be a boat by the shore. Where is it?"

But when he turned around, the Dwarf had already disappeared between the trees.

Will was staring at his reflection in the water. Jacob skimmed a stone across the dark surface, but his brother's reflection quickly returned, distorted and even more threatening.

"I nearly killed you back there, in the gorge." Will's voice sounded barely distinct from that of a Goyl now. "Look at me. No matter what you're hoping to find here, it's too late. You need to face it."

Clara was gazing at them. The Fairy magic clung to her like pollen. Only Will seemed immune. *Where's your brother, Jacob? Where did you leave him?* The rustling leaves sounded like their mother's voice.

Will backed away from Jacob, as though afraid he might strike him again.

"Let me go to them."

The sun was setting behind the trees, and its dying light spilled onto the lake like molten gold. The Fairy lilies opened their pale blossoms, welcoming the night.

Jacob pulled Will away from the water.

"You wait here, by the shore," he said. "Stay right here. I promise I'll be back soon."

The vixen pressed against his legs, her fur bristling as she looked at the island.

"What are you waiting for, Fox?" said Jacob. "Find me that boat."

26. THE RED FAIRY

Fox found the boat. And this time she didn't ask Jacob to take her along. However, just as he climbed in, she bit his hand so hard that the blood trickled down his fingers.

"That's so you won't forget me!" she snapped, and her eyes brimmed with the fear that she might lose him again.

Three years ago the Fairies had chased Fox

away after they'd found Jacob, half-dead, in their forest, and she had nearly drowned trying to follow them to the island. And yet she had waited for him, a whole year, while he forgot all about her and everything else. Now she sat there again, her fur blackened by the approaching night, even after he'd already rowed far out into the lake. Clara, too, stood among the willows, and this time even Will watched him go.

"It's too late for me." The waves lapping against the narrow boat seemed to echo Will's words, but who better to break the spell of the Dark Fairy than her sister? Jacob reached for the medallion on his chest. He had picked the petal inside on the day he'd left Miranda. It made him invisible to her, as if he'd cast off not only his love but also the body that had loved her. A petal, nothing more. She herself had told him that he could hide himself from her this way. When Fairies were in love, they revealed all their secrets in their sleep; you just had to ask the right questions.

Fortunately, the petal also made him invisible to the other Fairies. As he hid the boat in the reeds on the island's shore, Jacob saw four of them standing in the water. Their long hair floated on the surface as if the night itself had spun it. But Miranda was not among them. One of them looked his way, and Jacob was grateful for the thick carpet of flowers that made his steps as silent as Fox's paws. He had seen how they turned men into thistles or fish. The flowers were blue, like the bluebell Clara had picked, and not even the medallion could shield Jacob from the memories their scent evoked. *Careful, Jacob!* He dug his fingers into the bloody imprint Fox's teeth had left on his hand.

Soon he saw the first of the dark nets the moths of the Fairies spun between the trees. Tents as delicate as lacewing skin, that even in daytime stayed so dark they appeared to have trapped the night in their mesh. The Fairies only slept there when the sun was in the sky, but Jacob could think of no better place to wait for Miranda.

The Red Fairy. It was by that name that he had first heard mention of her. A drunk mercenary had told him about a friend she had lured to the island and who, after his return, had been so sick with yearning for her he had drowned himself. Everyone had heard such stories about the Fairies, though few ever got to see one. Some thought their island was actually the Realm of the Dead, but the Fairies knew nothing of human time or death. Miranda called the Dark Fairy her sister only because both of them had emerged from the lake on the same day. So how could she truly understand the despair he felt as his brother grew a skin of stone?

The tent, which for almost a year had been the beginning and the end of his world, clung to Jacob's clothes as he felt his way through its gauzy walls. His eyes adapted slowly to the darkness, and he was startled by the sight of a sleeping figure on the bed of moss where he himself had lain so often.

She hadn't changed. Of course not. Fairies didn't age. Her skin was as pale as the lilies on the lake, and her hair was as dark as the night she so loved. At night her eyes turned black, though by day they were as blue as the sky or as green as the water of the lake, mirroring the leaves of the willows. Too beautiful. Too beautiful for human eyes. Untouched by time and the decay it wrought. But in the end a man wants to sense the same mortality that dwells in his own flesh also in the skin he caresses.

Jacob pulled the medallion from his shirt and unhooked it from the chain around his neck. Miranda stirred as soon as he placed it next to her, and Jacob took a step back as she whispered his name in her dream. It wasn't a good dream, and she opened her eyes with a start.

So beautiful. Jacob's fingers sought the bite marks on his hand.

"Since when do you sleep away the night?"

For a moment she seemed to think he was still the dream that had woken her. But then she noticed the medallion lying next to her. She opened it and took out the petal.

"So that's how you hid yourself from me." Jacob wasn't sure what he saw on her face. Horror or joy. Love or hatred. Maybe something of it all. "Who told you how?"

"You did."

Her moths immediately swarmed at his face as he took a step toward her.

"You have to help me, Miranda."

She got up and brushed the moss from her skin.

"I used to sleep away the nights because they reminded me too much of you," she said. "But that was a long time ago. Now it's just a bad habit."

The wings of her moths tinged the night air red.

"I see you haven't come alone," she said, crumbling the lily petal between her fingers. "And you brought a Goyl."

"He's my brother." This time the moths let him approach her. "It's a Fairy's curse, Miranda."

"But you've come to the wrong Fairy."

"You must know a way to break it."

She seemed to be made of the shadows that surrounded her, of the moonlight and the night's dew on the leaves. He'd been so happy when this was all he knew. But there was so much more.

"My sister isn't one of us anymore." Miranda turned her back to him. "She betrayed us for the Goyl."

"Then help me!"

Jacob reached out his hand, but she pushed it away.

"Why should I?"

"I had to leave! I couldn't stay here forever."

"That's what my sister said. But Fairies don't leave. We belong to the place that brought us into this world. You knew that as well as she did."

So beautiful. The memories spun a web in the darkness, entangling them both.

"Help him, Miranda. Please!"

She raised her hand and brushed her fingers over his lips.

"Kiss me!"

It felt as if he were kissing the night, or the wind. Her moths were piercing his skin, and all he had lost tasted like ashes in his mouth. When he let her go, he thought for a brief moment he could see his own death in her eyes.

A fox was barking outside. Fox always claimed she could feel when he was in danger.

Miranda turned her back to him.

"There is only one remedy against this spell," she said.

"What is it?"

"You will have to destroy my sister."

Jacob's heart stopped, for one beat, and he felt his own fear clammy on his skin.

The Dark Fairy.

"She turns her enemies into the wine she drinks or into the iron from which her lover builds his bridges." Even Chanute's voice had sounded hoarse when he'd spoken of her.

"But she can't be killed," he said. "Any more than you can."

"For a Fairy, there are far worse things than death."

For a moment, her beauty was like a poisonous flower.

"How long does your brother have left?" she asked.

"Two, maybe three days."

Voices came to them through the dark. The other

Fairies. Jacob had never found out how many of them there were.

Miranda gazed at her bed as if remembering the times they had shared it. "My sister is with the Goyl, in his main fortress."

That was a ride of at least six days.

It would be too late. Much too late.

Jacob wasn't sure which he felt more, the despair or the relief.

Miranda reached out. One of her moths perched delicately on her finger.

"You can still make it if I give you some time."

Fox began to bark again.

"One of us once cursed a princess to die on her fifteenth birthday. But we suspended that curse. With a deep sleep."

In his mind's eye, Jacob saw the castle, wrapped in thorns, and the sleeping beauty in the bedchamber at the top of the tower....

"She died anyway," he said. "Nobody woke her."

Miranda shrugged. "I'll make your brother sleep. It's up to you to make sure he is awoken. But not before you have broken my sister's power."

The moth on her hand was preening its wings.

"The girl who is with you. She belongs to your brother?" Miranda brushed her naked foot over the ground, and the moonlight drew Clara's face on the dark earth.

"Yes," Jacob replied—and he felt something he didn't quite comprehend.

"Does she love him?"

"Yes," he said, "I think so."

"She'd better, for should she not, he will sleep himself to death." Miranda wiped away the moonlight image. "Have you ever met my sister?"

Jacob shook his head. He had seen blurry photographs, a sketch in a newspaper—the Demon Lover, the Fairy Witch, who makes stone grow in the flesh of humans. . . .

"She is the fairest of us all." Miranda's eyes traced the features of his face as if trying to recall the love she'd once felt. "Don't look at her for too long," she said softly. "And whatever she promises you, do exactly as I say, or your brother is lost."

Fox's bark rang through the night again. *I'm fine, Fox*, thought Jacob. *All will be well.* Even if he did not yet quite understand how.

He took Miranda's hand. Six fingers, as white as

the flowers on the lake. She let him kiss her again. "What if the price for my help is that you come back to me?" she whispered. "Would you do it?"

"Is that your price?" he asked, though he was terrified of the answer.

She smiled. "No," she said. "My price will be paid when you destroy my sister."

27. So Far Away

Will had not once taken his eyes off the island. It was painful for Clara to see the fear on his face—fear of himself and of what Jacob would learn on the island but, first and foremost, fear that his brother wouldn't come back, that he would be left alone with his skin of stone.

He had forgotten Clara. But she still went to

him. The stone didn't yet completely conceal the one she loved, and he was so alone.

"Jacob will be back soon, Will. I'm sure."

He didn't turn around.

"With Jacob, you never know when he'll come back," he said. "Believe me, I know what I'm talking about."

They were both here: the stranger from the cave, whose iciness she could still taste on her tongue like poison, and the other one, who had stood in the hospital corridor in front of his mother's room and smiled at her every time she walked past. Will. She missed him so much.

"He'll come back," she said. "I know it. And he'll find a way. He loves you. Even though he's not very good at showing it."

Will shook his head.

"You don't know him," he said, turning his back to the lake as though he was sick of seeing his reflection in the water. "Jacob has never been able to accept that not everything turns out right, that some things and some people just get lost."

He averted his face, as if remembering the jade. But Clara didn't see it. This was still the face she loved. The mouth she had kissed so often. Even the eyes were still his, despite the gold. But when she reached out, he shuddered, as he had done in the cave, and the night was like a black river running between them.

Will pulled from inside his coat the pistol that Jacob had given him.

"Here, take this," he said. "You may need it if Jacob doesn't come back and should I no longer remember your name tomorrow. If you have to kill him, the other one with the stone face, just remember that he has done the same to me."

She wanted to back away, but Will held on to her, pushing the gun into her hand. He avoided touching her skin, but he ran his fingers through her hair.

"I'm so sorry!" he whispered.

Then he stepped past her and disappeared beneath the willows. Clara stared at the pistol. Then she took a few steps toward the lake and hurled it into the dark water.

28. JUST A ROSE

Jacob stayed the whole night, though every hour tasted of ash. He loosened Miranda's black hair from the darkness and sought solace in her white skin. He allowed his fingers to remember and his mind to forget. Outside, the other Fairies laughed and whispered, and Jacob wondered whether she would protect him should they discover him. He didn't really care.

That night, nothing mattered. No tomorrow. No yesterday. No brother and no father. Just black hair and white skin and red wings writing words he didn't understand into the dark night.

But when even the canopy could no longer shield them from the day, the bite on his hand started to throb, and everything flooded back: the fear, the stone, the gold in Will's eyes—and the hope that he might yet have found a way to put an end to it all.

Miranda didn't ask him whether he would come back. But before he left, she made him repeat everything she'd taught him about her dark sister. Word for word.

Brother. Sister.

The lilies were already closing in the first rays of the sun. Jacob saw none of the other Fairies as he returned to the boat, but the froth drifting on the lake heralded that soon the water would give birth to another.

Will was nowhere to be seen as Jacob rowed back toward the lake's shore, but Clara was asleep between the willows. She woke with a start as he pushed the boat ashore. After the beauty of the Fairies, her tired face resembled a wildflower beside a bouquet of lilies.

But she didn't seem to mind the leaves in her hair, or her dirty clothes. All Jacob saw on Clara's face was relief that he was back—and fear for his brother. *"Your brother will need her. And you will, too."* Fox had once again been right. She always was, and luckily this time he had listened to her.

She came out from under the willow branches, her fur bristling, as though she knew exactly why he'd returned only now.

"That was a long night," she said testily. "I'd started checking the fish to see if there was one that looked like you."

"I'm back, aren't I?" Jacob retorted. "And she'll help him."

"Why?"

"Why? Does it matter? Because she can. Because she doesn't like her sister. I don't really care, as long as she does it."

Fox stared across the lake, her eyes narrowed with suspicion. Clara, however, looked so relieved that all the weariness vanished from her face.

"When?" she asked.

"Soon."

Fox could tell from his face that there was more to

it, but she kept quiet. She knew she wouldn't like the whole truth. Clara was too happy to notice any of this.

"Fox thought you'd forgotten about us." Will stepped out from under the willows, and for an instant Jacob thought he'd stayed too long on the island. The jade had darkened. It merged with the green of the trees. The world behind the mirror had finally turned Will into a part of it. It had sown its seed in his flesh, like a parasite laying its eggs in the body of a caterpillar, and now it stared at Jacob with golden eyes, gripping his brother in its fangs. But he would free him with the same weapon the Mirrorworld had used against him: the words of a Fairy.

"We have to find a rose," Jacob said.

"A rose? That's it?" The jade face was impassive. So familiar and yet so strange.

"Yes, it grows not far from here." *And then, brother, you will sleep, and I'll have to find the Dark Fairy.*

"You can't just make it disappear." The way Will looked at him! As if he'd forgotten and yet remembered everything that had driven them apart.

"Can't I?" Jacob replied. "I know that she can help you. Just do what I tell you, and everything will be all right."

Fox wouldn't take her eyes off him. They were saying, *What are you trying to do, Jacob Reckless? You are scared.*

So what, Fox? he wanted to reply. *It's a feeling I've gotten quite used to by now.*

29. In the Heart

They rode northward along the lakeshore. Time drowned in the scent of the blossoms, in the light breaking on the water, and for the first time Clara felt ready to forgive this world for all the fear and all the gloom. Everything would be all right. Everything.

Jacob soon turned his back to the lake. The horses sank deep into the vines of the brambles

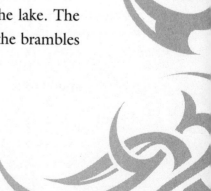

and the fronds of the ferns. Above them the leaves were again turning yellow. A cool wind rushed through the branches, and beyond the trees Clara could already see the valley where the Unicorns grazed. They were still far, barely visible in the mist that hung between the mountains. But their dead kin lay at Clara's feet in the yellow grass.

Their skeletons were everywhere, moss and grass between their ribs, spiderwebs spanning their hollow eye sockets, the white horns still on their bare-boned foreheads. The Unicorns' graveyard. Maybe they came here to die because it was easier under the canopy of the branches, or because in death they sought to be near the Fairies. Vines with tiny white blossoms wove their tendrils through the bleached bones, like a final salute from the Fairies to their faithful guards.

Jacob dismounted and approached one of the skeletons. A single red rose was growing out of its chest.

"Will, come here." He waved his brother to his side.

Fox ran under the trees and peered toward the Unicorns, her muzzle raised in the breeze.

"I smell Goyl."

"So? Will's right behind you." Jacob turned his back to the valley. "Pick the rose, Will."

Will put out his hand—and drew it back again. He looked at his jade-green fingers. Then he looked at Clara, searching her face for the one he had once been.

Please, Will. She didn't say it, but she thought it, again and again. *Do what your brother says!* And here, among the flowers and the dead, for one precious moment, he looked at her as he once used to. *All will be well.*

He picked the rose, and Clara heard the woody stem snap. One of its thorns pricked his finger, and Will looked in surprise at the pale amber blood oozing from his petrified skin.

He dropped the rose and rubbed his forehead.

"What is this?" he said, faltering and looking at his brother. "What have you done?"

Clara reached out to him, but Will flinched away from her, stumbling over one of the skeletons. The bones cracked like rotten wood under his boots.

"Will, listen!" Jacob grabbed his arm. "You have to sleep. I need more time. When you wake up, all this will be over. I promise."

But Will shoved him away with such violence that

Jacob staggered back, out of the shelter of the trees into the open expanse of the autumnal meadow.

"Jacob!" Fox yelped. "Come back under the trees!"

The image would stay with Clara forever. Jacob, looking back. And then the gunshot.

Such a sharp sound. Like wood splintering.

The bullet struck Jacob's chest.

Fox cried out as he fell on the yellow grass. Will ran to him before Clara could hold him back. He dropped to his knees next to his brother, calling his name, but Jacob didn't move. Blood stained his shirt right above his heart.

The Goyl appeared out of the mist like a bad dream, still holding the rifle. He was limping, and his left arm seemed to be injured as well. One of his soldiers was by his side—the girl Jacob had shot as she attacked Clara with her saber. Her uniform was still soaked with her colorless blood.

Fox leaped at them with bared fangs, but the Goyl just kicked her out of the way. The vixen shifted shape, the pain robbing her of her fur. Clara wrapped her arms protectively around Fox as she cowered into the grass, sobbing. Will got to his feet, his face ablaze with rage. He reached the rifle Jacob had dropped, but he stumbled groggily, and the Goyl grabbed him and pressed the gun to his temple.

"Easy now!" he said while the She-Goyl pointed her pistol at Clara. "I had a score to settle with your brother, but we won't harm a hair on you."

Fox struggled out of Clara's embrace and pulled the pistol from Jacob's belt. The She-Goyl kicked it out of her hand while Will just stood there, staring down at his brother.

"Look at him, Nesser," the Goyl said, roughly turning Will's face toward him. "He really is turning jade."

Will tried to ram his head into the Goyl's face, but he was too numbed. The Goyl laughed.

"You're one of us, all right!" he said. "Even if you can't accept it yet. Tie his hands!" he ordered the She-Goyl. Then he went over to Jacob's body and examined him as a hunter would his prey.

"His face looks familiar. What's his name?" he asked Will.

Will didn't answer.

"Never mind," the Goyl said, turning away. "You Doughskins all look the same, anyway. Round up the horses," he barked at the girl. Then he pushed Will toward Jacob's mare.

"Where are you taking him?" Clara barely recognized her own voice.

The Goyl didn't even turn around.

"Forget him!" he said over his shoulder. "He will soon forget you."

30. A Shroud of Red Bodies

The gunshot wound looked much less harmful than the wounds Jacob had suffered when the Unicorns tore open his back. Back then, however, Jacob had been breathing, and Fox had felt his faint pulse. Now he was just still.

So much pain. She wanted to dig her teeth into her flesh just not to feel it anymore. Her

fur wouldn't come back, and she felt as exposed and lost as an abandoned child.

Clara was cowering next to her in the grass, her arms clasped around her knees. She shed no tears. She just sat there, as if someone had cut out her heart.

Clara was the first to see the Dwarf. He was wading toward them through the grass, looking as innocent as if they'd caught him picking mushrooms. However, who else but a Dwarf could have told the Goyl that the only way out of the Fairy realm was through the Unicorn graveyard?

Fox wiped the tears from her eyes and felt through the grass for Jacob's pistol.

"Stop! Stop! What are you doing?" Valiant yelled as she pointed the weapon at him. He quickly cowered behind the nearest bush. "How could I know they'd shoot him right away? I thought they just wanted his brother."

Clara got to her feet.

"Shoot him, Fox," she said. "If you don't, I will."

"Wait!" Valiant clamored. "They caught me on my way back to the gorge. What was I supposed to do? Get myself killed as well?"

"And now?" Fox yelled at him. "Come to plunder a corpse on your way back?"

"That's outrageous! I'm here to rescue you!" the Dwarf retorted with genuine indignation. "Two girls, all alone, lost and helpless..."

"So helpless that we'll surely pay you to save us?"

The silence answering from the bush was very telling, and Fox lifted the pistol again. If only she could stop the tears. They blurred everything: the misty valley, the bush where the treacherous Dwarf was hiding, and Jacob's lifeless face.

"Fox!"

Clara put a hand on her arm. A red moth had landed on Jacob's punctured chest. Another landed on his brow.

Fox dropped the pistol.

"Get away from him!" she shouted, her voice drowning in tears. "Go and tell your mistress he's never coming back!" She leaned over Jacob. "Didn't I tell you," she whispered, "not to go back to the Fairies? This time it will kill you."

Another moth landed on the still body. More and more of them fluttered out of the trees. They settled on him in such profusion that they looked like flowers sprouting from his shattered flesh.

Fox tried to drive the moths away, but there were too many. Finally she gave up and simply watched as they covered Jacob with their wings. It was as if the Red Fairy was claiming him even in death.

Clara knelt next to Fox and wrapped her arms around her.

"We have to bury him."

Fox freed herself from Clara's embrace and pressed her face against Jacob's chest.

Bury him.

"I'll do it." The Dwarf had actually dared to venture closer. He picked up the rifle Jacob had dropped, and as if the metal were as soft as clay, he slapped the barrel flat with his bare hand, shaping it into a spade. "Bloody waste!" he muttered as he attacked the soil. "Two pounds of red moonstone! And now nobody will get it."

The Dwarf dug the grave effortlessly, as if he'd had a lot of practice. Fox just sat there, her arms wrapped around Clara, and looked at Jacob's still face. The moths were still covering him like a shroud when Valiant threw down his shovel and brushed the dirt off his hands.

"Right," he said. "Let's get him in there." He leaned over Jacob. "But first we should check his pockets. No point in letting perfectly good gold sovereigns rot in the ground."

Fox's fur returned in an instant. "Don't touch him!" she hissed, snapping at Valiant's eager fingers.

Bite him, Fox. As hard as you can. Maybe that will ease the pain.

The Dwarf tried to fend her off with the shovel-rifle, but she tore into his coat and jumped at his throat until Clara grabbed her by her fur and pulled her back.

"Fox, don't!" she whispered, pressing the quivering body against hers. "He's right. We'll need the money. And Jacob's weapons. The compass... everything he had with him."

"Why?"

"To find Will."

What was she talking about?

Behind them the Dwarf snorted in disbelief. "Will? There is no more Will."

But Clara bent over Jacob and put her hand in his coat pocket. "We'll give you all he had—if you help us find his brother," she said. "That's what he would've wanted."

She pulled the handkerchief from Jacob's pocket. Two gold sovereigns dropped onto his chest. The moths swirled up like leaves stirred by an autumn breeze.

"Strange how little resemblance there was between

the two," Clara said, brushing the dark hair from Jacob's forehead. "Do you have sisters, Fox?"

"Three brothers."

Fox rubbed her head against Jacob's lifeless hand. A last moth rose from his chest. Suddenly she flinched. His body shuddered—his lips gasped for air, and his hands clawed into the grass.

Jacob!

Fox impulsively jumped on his chest, causing him to groan with pain.

No grave. No damp soil on his face! She bit his chin and his cheeks. Oh, she just wanted to eat him up with love.

"Fox. What are you doing?" He grabbed her and sat up.

Clara backed away from him as if from a ghost. The Dwarf dropped his shovel.

But Jacob sat there and looked at his bloody shirt.

"Whose blood is this?"

"Yours!" Fox nestled against his chest to feel his heartbeat. "The Goyl shot you."

Jacob looked at her incredulously. Then he unbuttoned his blood-soaked shirt. But instead of a wound, there was only the pale red imprint of a moth on the skin above his heart.

"You were dead, Jacob." Clara struggled with the words, as if her tongue had to search for every syllable. "Dead."

Jacob touched the mark on his chest. He wasn't all there yet; Fox could see it in his eyes. But finally he looked around.

"Where's Will?"

Jacob struggled to his feet as he noticed the Dwarf standing behind him.

Valiant gave him his broadest smile. "That Fairy must have really taken quite a fancy to you! I heard they sometimes bring their lovers back from the dead, but that they also do that for the ones who ran out on them...." He shook his head and picked up the warped rifle.

"Where's my brother?" Jacob took a step toward the Dwarf, but Valiant managed to evade him with a quick leap across the empty grave.

"Easy, now!" he called, waving the rifle at Jacob. "How am I supposed to tell you if you wring my neck?"

Clara pushed the handkerchief and the gold sovereigns back into Jacob's pocket. "I'm sorry. I didn't know how to find Will without you." She pressed her face against his shoulder. "I thought I'd lost you both!"

"Don't worry." Jacob stroked her hair soothingly, all the while keeping his eyes fixed on Valiant. "We'll find Will. I promise. We don't need the Dwarf for that."

"Really?" Valiant snapped the bent barrel off the rifle as if it were a brittle twig. "They're taking your brother to the royal fortress. The last human who tried to sneak in there was an imperial spy. They cast him in amber and put him on display right next to the main gate. Terrible sight."

Jacob picked up his pistol and pushed it back into his belt. "But of course you know a way to get in."

Valiant's mouth stretched into such a smug grin that Fox bared her teeth. "Of course."

Jacob eyed the Dwarf as if he were a poisonous snake.

"How much?"

Valiant bent the broken rifle into shape.

"That gold tree you sold to the Empress last year. Word is you kept a cutting."

Fortunately, Valiant missed the look Fox shot at Jacob. There was indeed a cutting. It grew behind the ruin, by the scorched stables, but the only gold it had yielded so far was its foul-smelling pollen. Still, Jacob managed to produce an expression of honest indignation.

"That's an outrageous price!"

"Appropriate is more the word." Valiant's eyes were glinting as if he could already feel the gold raining down on his shoulders. "And the vixen has to take me to it even if you don't make it out of the fortress alive. I want your word of honor on it."

"Honor?" Fox growled. "I'm surprised that word doesn't make your lips blister."

The Dwarf leered at her. Jacob, however, held out his hand to him.

"Give him your word, Fox," he said. "No matter what happens, he'll have earned himself that tree."

31. Dark Glass

Without the horses, it took them hours to reach a road that led from the valley up into the mountains, and Jacob had to carry Valiant on his back so the Dwarf wouldn't slow them down even more. Finally a farmer gave them a lift on his cart to the next village, where Jacob bought two new horses, and a donkey for the Dwarf. The horses weren't fast, but at least they

were used to the steep mountain paths, and Jacob only stopped when the darkness made them lose their way.

He found a spot beneath a rocky outcrop that gave some protection from the cold wind. Soon Valiant was snoring as loudly as if he were in one of the soft beds for which Dwarf inns were famous. Fox scampered off to hunt, and Jacob advised Clara to bed down next to the horses so that they would keep her warm. Then he lit a fire with some dry wood he'd found among the rocks, and tried to regain some of the calm he had felt on the island. Again and again, he caught himself touching the dried blood on his shirt, but all he remembered was Will's accusing stare after he'd been pricked by the rose, and then a relieved Fox nudging his face with her muzzle. In between there was nothing, just an echo of pain and darkness.

And his brother was gone.

"When you wake up, all this will be over. I promise."

How, Jacob? Even if the Dwarf didn't double-cross him again. Even if he managed to find the Dark Fairy in the fortress. How was he going to get close enough to touch her, let alone utter what he'd learned from her sister, before she could kill him? *Don't think, Jacob. Just go.*

He felt a searing impatience, as if death had only increased his old restlessness.

Ride, Jacob. Onward, just as you've done for years. The wind drove into the flames, and he buttoned his coat over his bloody shirt.

"Jacob?"

Clara was standing behind him. She had wrapped a horse blanket around her shoulders, and he noticed that her hair had grown longer.

"How are you feeling?" In her voice Jacob still heard the disbelief that he was actually alive.

"Fine," he answered. "Would you like to check my pulse? Just to make sure?"

She had to smile, but the concern in her eyes remained.

An owl was screaming above them. In this world, owls were regarded as the souls of dead Witches. Clara knelt next to him on the cold earth and held her hands above the warming flames.

"Do you still think you can help Will?"

She looked terribly tired.

"Yes," he said. "And trust me, you don't want to know more than that. It would just scare you."

When she looked at him, her eyes were as blue as Will's. Before they had drowned in gold.

"Is that the reason you didn't tell Will why he had to pick that rose?" The wind blew sparks into her hair. "I think your brother knows more about fear than you do."

Words. Nothing more. But they turned the night into dark glass in which Jacob saw himself.

"I know why you're here." Clara's voice sounded distant, as though she were speaking not about him but about herself. "This world doesn't frighten you half as much as the other one. You have nothing and nobody to lose here. Except Fox, and she clearly worries more about you than you do about her. You've left all that could frighten you in the other world. But then Will came here and brought it all with him."

She got up again and wiped the earth off her knees.

"Whatever you're planning, please be careful. Getting yourself killed for Will won't make up for anything. But if there is a way, any way, to turn him back into who he was, then let me help! Even if you think it'll frighten me. You're not the only one who doesn't want to lose him. Why else would I still be here?"

Clara walked off before Jacob could answer. He wished her far away. And he was glad she wasn't. And he saw his face in the dark glass of the night. Undistorted. Just as she had drawn it.

32. THE RIVER

It took them another four days to reach the mountains the Goyl called home.

Frosty days, cold nights. Rain and damp clothes. One of the horses lost a shoe, and the blacksmith they took it to told Clara about a Bluebeard who had bought three girls, barely older than her, from their fathers in a nearby village and had taken them to his castle and

murdered them. Clara listened impassively, but Jacob could tell from her expression that by now she considered her own story to be almost as horrific.

"What's she still doing here?" Valiant asked in a whisper one morning while the bone-weary Clara struggled to mount her horse. "The things you humans do to your females. She belongs in a house. Nice dresses, servants, cakes, a soft bed—that's what she needs."

"And a Dwarf for a husband, and a golden lock on her door to which only you have the key," Jacob retorted.

"And why not?" Valiant replied, giving Clara his most ravishing smile.

The nights were so cold that they stayed in inns. Clara shared her bed with Fox, and Jacob slept next to the snoring Dwarf. But that was not the only reason he slept badly. In his dreams he was smothered by red moths, and he would wake up drenched in sweat, tasting his own blood in his mouth.

On the evening of the fourth day, they saw the first of the towers the Goyl had built along their borders. Slender stalagmites with fibrous walls and windows of onyx, but Valiant knew a path through the mountains to avoid them.

For centuries the Goyl had been just one of the terrors of these lands, mentioned in the same breath as Ogres and Brown Wolves. All along, their worst crime had been to look too human. They were the despised twins, stone cousins who dwelled in the dark. Nowhere had they been hunted as mercilessly as in the mountains they came from, and now the Goyl were paying back in kind; it was in their old homeland that their rule was most merciless.

Valiant avoided the highways used by their troops, but they still kept meeting Goyl patrols. The Dwarf introduced Jacob and Clara as rich clients who were planning to build a glass factory near the royal fortress. Jacob had bought Clara one of the gold-embroidered skirts worn by the rich women of the area, and he had swapped his own clothes for those of a wealthy merchant. He barely recognized himself in the fur-collared coat and the soft gray trousers. Riding had become even more cumbersome for Clara in the wide skirt, but at least the Goyl always waved them past after Valiant had told them his story.

On an evening that already carried the scent of snow, they finally reached the river beyond which the royal fortress lay. The ferry crossing was in Blenheim, a town the Goyl had taken many years before. Nearly half the houses had bricked-up windows. The conquerors had even canopied many of the roads to protect themselves from the sun. And behind the harbor wall there was a heavily guarded manhole, indicating that this town now also had an underground district.

Fox disappeared between the houses to catch herself one of the scrawny chickens that were pecking at the cobblestones. Jacob walked with Valiant and Clara across the square toward the ferry landing. The evening sky was glistening on the murky waters, and on the opposite shore he could see a rectangular gate gaping in the mountainside.

"Is that the entrance to the fortress?" Jacob asked the Dwarf.

But Valiant shook his head. "No. No. That's just one of the cave cities they built aboveground after the fortress got too crowded. What you want is farther inland, and it lies so deep underground that you'll wish you could unlearn to breathe."

Jacob tethered the horses and walked with Clara toward the jetty. The ferryman was already padlocking his boat. He looked nearly as hideous as the Trolls in the north, who were constantly being frightened by their own reflections. His boat had also seen better days. The shallow hull was clad in iron, and when

Jacob asked the ferryman whether he could take them across before nightfall, his face warped into a scornful grin.

"This river ain't a very hospi'able place after dark." He spoke so loudly, as if he wanted to be heard clear across the river. "And as of tomorrow, all crossings are to be suspended because the crowned Goyl will emerge from his den to go to his wedding."

"Wedding?" Valiant shrugged in response to Jacob's puzzled look.

"Where have you been?" the ferryman sneered. "Your Empress is giving him her daughter to buy peace from the stone faces. Tomorrow they'll swarm out of their holes like termites, and the Goyl will ride to Vena on his Devil-train and take the 'Loveliest Princess in the Land' with him to his burrow."

"Will the Fairy go with him?"

Valiant cast Jacob a curious glance.

The ferryman, however, just shrugged. "Sure. The Goyl goes nowhere without her. Not even when he marries another woman."

Once again, time is running out on you, Jacob.

Jacob put his hand in his pocket. "Did you take a Goyl officer across today?"

"What?" The ferryman held a hand behind his ear.

"A Goyl officer. Jasper skin? Nearly blind in one eye. He had a prisoner with him."

The ferryman shot a sideways glance at the Goyl sentry by the wall, but the soldier was out of earshot and had his back turned to them. "Why? You one of them headhunters?" The ferryman had lowered his voice, but he was still speaking so loudly that now it was Jacob's turn to cast a worried glance at the sentry. "His prisoner would fetch you a fine price. He had a color I ain't seen on any of them yet."

Jacob would have loved to punch his ugly face. Instead, he pulled a gold sovereign from his handkerchief. "You'll get another one on the other side—if you take us across tonight."

The ferryman eyed the coin greedily, but Valiant grabbed Jacob's arm and pulled him aside. "Let's wait until tomorrow," he hissed at him. "It's getting dark, and this river is swarming with Lorelei."

Lorelei. Jacob looked at the languid water. His grandfather had sometimes sung him a song about Lorelei. The words had made him shudder as a child, but the stories told about the Lorelei in this world were even more sinister.

Still.

He didn't have much choice.

"No worries!" The ferryman put out his calloused hand. "We won't wake them."

But once Jacob had dropped the gold sovereign into his palm, the ferryman reached into his baggy pockets, handing him and Valiant each a pair of wax earplugs, which looked distinctly as if they had been used before.

"Just to be on the safe side," he said. "You never know."

He flashed Clara a sly grin.

"You won't need them. The Lorelei are only after us men."

Fox came running down the jetty as they led the horses onto the ferry. She licked a few feathers from her fur before jumping aboard the shallow boat. The horses were restless, but the ferryman pushed the gold coins into his pocket and untied the ropes.

The ferry drifted out onto the river. Behind them the houses of Blenheim dissolved into the twilight, and the only sound was the lapping of the water against the metal-clad hull. The opposite shore was slowly coming closer, and the ferryman gave Jacob a wink. But the horses were still restless, and Fox was standing with pricked ears.

A voice wafted across the water.

At first it sounded like a bird singing, but then more and more like a woman's voice. The voice was coming from the direction of the rocks that protruded from the water to their left, gray boulders that made it seem as if the twilight itself had been turned to stone. A shape moved on the rock and slid into the water. A second followed. And then they were everywhere.

Valiant uttered a curse. "What did I tell you?" he hissed at Jacob. "Faster!" he shouted at the ferryman. "Come on!"

The man seemed to hear neither the Dwarf nor the voices that drifted ever more enticingly across the water. It was only when Jacob put a hand on his shoulder that he spun around.

"He can't hear!" Valiant screamed, already stuffing the wax into his ears. "That cunning dog is nearly as deaf as a dead fish!"

The ferryman just shrugged and clutched his oar more tightly. Jacob, pushing the grimy earplugs into his ears, wondered how often the ferryman had come back without his passengers.

The horses shied. Jacob could barely control them. The last daylight was fading, and the shore inched toward them so painfully slowly, as if the water was dragging them back again. Clara stood close by Jacob's side, and Fox posted herself protectively in front of him, though he could see that her fur was bristling with fear. The voices grew so loud that Jacob could hear them through the earplugs, luring him into the water. Clara pulled him back from the guard-rail, but the singing seeped through his skin like sweet venom. Heads emerged from the waves, hair drifting on the water like spun gold, and as Clara let go of him for one second to press her hands over her own aching ears, Jacob felt his fingers reaching for the protective wax, pulling it out of his ears and throwing it overboard.

The singing ran through his brain like honey-coated knives. Clara tried to hold him back as he staggered toward the edge of the ferry, but Jacob shoved her away so hard that she stumbled against the ferryman.

Where were they? Jacob leaned over the water, and at first he saw only his own reflection, but then it melted into a face. It looked like the face of a woman except it didn't have a nose. The eyes were silver, and fangs pushed over the pale green lips. Arms reached out of the river, and fingers closed around Jacob's wrist. Another hand grabbed his hair. Water lapped into the ferry. They were everywhere, reaching out for him, their scaly bodies pushed halfway out of the water, their teeth bared. Lorelei. Much worse than the song. Reality always was so much worse.

Fox dug her teeth into one of the scaly arms that had grabbed him, but the other Lorelei were already pulling Jacob over the guardrail. He struggled against them, but finally he lost his footing. Then he heard a shot, and the mermaid sank back into the murky water, a gaping hole in her head.

Clara was standing behind him, holding the pistol he had given her. She shot another Lorelei who tried to pull the Dwarf into the water. The ferryman got two with a knife, and Jacob himself killed one that had struck her claws into Fox's hide. As the dead bodies drifted through the water, the other Lorelei backed off and set about devouring their dead kin.

The sight made Clara drop the pistol. She buried her face in her hands while Jacob and Valiant calmed the panicked horses and helped the ferryman steer the wildly pitching boat toward the jetty. The Lorelei screamed after them, but now their voices merely sounded like a swarm of shrieking gulls.

They were still howling as Jacob led the horses ashore. The ferryman stepped in his way and held out his hand. Valiant shoved him so hard that the man nearly stumbled into the river.

"Oh, so you did hear the bit about the second sovereign, did you?" the Dwarf yelled at him. "How about you give us back the first one, or do you always get paid for delivering dinner to the Lorelei?"

"What do you want? I took you across!" the ferryman merely retorted. "That damn Fairy put them in the river. Am I supposed to let her ruin my business? A deal's a deal."

"All right, then." Jacob produced another gold sovereign from his pocket. They were on the other side, and that was all that mattered. "But is there anything else we should be on the lookout for?"

Valiant's eyes followed the coin until it disappeared in the ferryman's grimy pocket.

"Did the Dwarf tell you about the Dragons? They're as red as the fire they spit. Whenever they fly over the mountains, you can see the fires they leave behind on the slopes for days."

"I did hear about that." Valiant gave Jacob a knowing look. "Don't you also tell your children that there are Giants on this side of the river? Superstitious twaddle." The Dwarf lowered his voice. "But should I tell you where there really are Dragons?"

The ferryman reflexively leaned down closer to the Dwarf.

"Saw it with my own eyes!" Valiant shouted into his deaf ear. "Sitting on its nest of bones, just two miles upriver from here. But it was a green one, and it had a leg as scrawny as yours dangling from its ugly mouth. And I said to myself, 'By the Devil and all his golden hairs,' I said, 'I wouldn't like to be in Blenheim the day that beast decides to fly downstream.'"

The ferryman's eyes grew as big as one of Jacob's gold sovereigns. "Two miles?" He cast a worried glance up the river.

"Yep, maybe even a little less." Valiant dropped the grimy earplugs into his hands. "Good luck on the return journey!"

"Not a bad story!" Jacob whispered as the Dwarf swung himself onto his donkey. "But what would you say if I told you that I really did see a Dragon once?"

"I'd say that you're a liar," the Dwarf replied under his breath.

Behind them the Lorelei were still screaming, and Jacob noticed some claw marks on Clara's arm as he helped her onto her horse. But he saw nothing in her eyes to suggest that she blamed him for forcing the crossing.

"What do you smell, Fox?" he asked.

"Goyl," she replied, "nothing but Goyl. As if the air is made of them."

33. So Tired

Will wanted to sleep. Just sleep and forget the blood, all that blood on Jacob's chest. He'd lost all sense of time, just as he could no longer feel his own skin or his own heart. His dead brother. That was the only image that found its way into his dreams. And the voices. One was rough. The other like water. Cool, dark water.

"Open your eyes," she said. But he couldn't.

He just wanted to sleep.

Even if it meant seeing all that blood.

A hand stroked his face. Not stone. Soft and cool.

"Wake up, Will."

But he only wanted to wake up when he was back in his world, where the blood on Jacob's chest would be nothing but a dream, as would the jade skin and the stranger stirring inside him.

"He was with your red sister."

The voice of the murderer. Will wanted to dig his new claws into the jasper skin, wanted to see him lying there, motionless like Jacob. But sleep held him prisoner, restraining his limbs more effectively than any fetters.

"When?" Rage. Will felt it like ice through every word. "Why did you not stop him?"

"How? You never told us how to get past the Unicorns." Hatred. Like ice meeting fire. "You are more powerful than she is. Just reverse whatever she did to him."

"This is a thorn spell. Nobody can reverse it. I saw he had a girl with him. Where is she?"

"I had no orders to bring her here."

The girl. What had she looked like? Will no longer knew. The blood had washed away her face.

"Bring her to me. Your King's life depends on it."

Will felt the fingers on his skin again. So soft and cool.

"A shield of jade. Made from the flesh of his enemies." Her voice stroked his face. "My dreams never lie."

34. LARKS' WATER

For a while, Valiant led them quite resolutely through the night. However, as the slopes around them became more rugged and the road they'd followed from the river petered out into scrub and rubble, he brought his donkey to a halt and looked around, obviously perplexed.

"What?" Jacob rode to his side. "Don't tell me you're already lost!"

"The last time I was here was in broad daylight!" the Dwarf retorted testily. "How am I supposed to find a hidden entrance when it's darker here than up a Giant's backside? It's got to be right here somewhere."

Jacob dismounted and handed the Dwarf his flashlight. "Take this!" he said. "Find the entrance. And sometime tonight would be good."

The Dwarf swept the darkness with the beam of the light. "What's this?" he asked incredulously. "Fairy magic?"

"Something like that," replied Jacob.

Valiant shone the flashlight down the shrubby slope. "I'd bet my hat it's down there somewhere." Fox eyed the Dwarf suspiciously as he stomped off down the hill.

"Better go with him," Jacob said. "He might get lost."

She wasn't too keen on the idea, but she quickly scampered after Valiant.

Clara dismounted and tied her horse to a nearby tree. The golden threads in her skirt shimmered even more brightly in the moonlight. Jacob plucked a few leaves from an oak tree and handed them to her.

"Rub these between your hands and then brush them over the embroidery."

Clara obeyed, and the threads dissolved under her fingers as if she'd wiped the gold off the fabric.

"Elven thread," Jacob said. "Very pretty, but any Goyl would spot you miles off."

Clara ran her fingers through her conspicuously fair hair as if trying to dull its color, like the dress.

"You're planning on going into the fortress alone, aren't you?"

"Yes. I am."

"If you'd been alone on the river, you'd be dead now. Let me come with you. Please."

But Jacob shook his head. "It's too dangerous. And Will would be lost if something happened to you. He'll soon need you a lot more than he'll need me."

"Why?" It was so cold that her breath hung in the air in white wisps.

"You'll have to wake him."

"Wake him?"

It took her a few moments to understand.

"The rose!"

And the prince bent over her and woke her with a kiss.

Above them, the crescents of the two moons looked like they had been starved by the night.

"What makes you think I can wake him? Your brother doesn't love me anymore!" She tried hard to hide the pain in her voice.

Jacob took off the coat that made him look like a merchant. The only humans in the fortress were slaves, and they definitely didn't wear fur-lined collars.

"But you love him," he said. "It'll have to do."

Clara was just standing there.

"What if not?" she said eventually.

"What if it's not enough?"

Jacob didn't have to answer. They both remembered the castle and the dead under the leaves.

"How long did it take Will to pluck up the courage to ask you out?" He slipped back into his old coat.

The memory wiped the fear off Clara's face. "Two weeks. I thought he never would. Although we ran into each other every day in the hospital, when he was visiting your mother."

"Two weeks? That was quick for Will!" Something rustled in the bushes. Jacob reached for his gun, but it was just a badger weaving its way through the brush. "Where did he take you?"

"To the hospital cafeteria. Not the most romantic

of places." Clara smiled. "He told me about this stray dog he'd found. He brought it to our next date." Jacob caught himself envying Will the expression on her face.

"Let's look for some water," he said.

They soon found a small pond. Next to it stood an abandoned farmer's cart. The wheels had sunk into the muddy bank, and a heron had built its nest on the rotting wooden bed. The horses greedily lapped at the clear water, and Valiant's donkey waded in to its knees. But when Clara knelt down to drink, Jacob pulled her back.

"Watermen," he said. "The cart probably belonged to some farm girl. They love to catch themselves human brides. And around here, they've probably been waiting a long time for their next victim."

Clara backed away from the pond, and Jacob thought he could hear a Waterman's sigh. They were vile creatures, but at least they didn't eat their victims, as the Lorelei did. Watermen dragged the girls into a cave, fed them, and brought them presents. Shells, pearls, jewelry from people who had drowned...For a while, Jacob had worked for the desperate parents of such abductees. He'd brought three girls back to the surface—poor deranged creatures who'd never quite returned from the dark caves where, surrounded by fish bones and pearls, they'd had to endure the slimy kisses of an infatuated Waterman. In one case, the parents had refused to pay him, because they no longer recognized their daughter.

Jacob left the horses to drink and went to search for the brook that fed the pond. He soon found it, a thin trickle that emerged from a crack in the nearby rocks. Jacob fished some dead leaves off the surface, and Clara filled her cupped hand with the ice-cold water. It tasted earthy and fresh. Jacob only saw the birds after both he and Clara had taken their first sips. Two dead larks, pressed against each other among the wet pebbles. He spat out the water and yanked Clara to her feet.

"What's the matter?" she asked, alarmed.

Her skin smelled of autumn and the wind. *Don't, Jacob.* But it was too late. Clara didn't flinch as he pulled her close. He grabbed her hair, kissed her mouth, and he felt her heart beating as fast as his own. The tiny hearts of the larks had burst from the madness. Hence the name: Larks' Water. Innocent, cool, and clear, but just one sip and you were lost. *Let her go, Jacob.* But he kissed her again, and it was his name she whispered, not Will's.

"Jacob!"

Woman and vixen—for one moment Fox was both. But it was the vixen who bit him so hard that he finally let go of Clara, though every fiber of his being wanted to hold her.

Clara stumbled back and wiped her mouth as though she could wipe away his kisses.

"Will you look at that!" Valiant pointed the flashlight at them and gave Jacob a lecherous smile. "Does this mean we can forget about saving your brother?"

Fox looked at him as if he'd kicked her.

Human and animal. Vixen and woman. She still seemed both at the same time. But she was all fox as she approached the stream and looked at the dead birds.

"Since when are you dumb enough to drink Larks' Water?"

"Dammit, Fox, it was dark!" His heart was still beating wildly.

"Larks' Water?" Clara didn't look at him. Her hands were shaking as she pushed the hair from her face. She did not look at him.

"Yes. Awful." Valiant gave her a theatrical smile of sympathy. "Once you've drunk from it, you happily jump on even the ugliest girl. Doesn't really work on

Dwarfs. Pity it was he, not I," he added with a sardonic glance at Jacob.

"How long will it last?" Clara's voice was barely audible.

"Some say it wears off after one attack. But there are those who believe it lasts for months. The Witches"—Valiant gave Jacob a salacious smile—"believe it only brings out what's already in your heart."

"You seem to know a lot about Larks' Water. Do you bottle the stuff and sell it?" Jacob barked at the Dwarf.

Valiant shrugged regretfully. "It doesn't keep. And the effect is too unpredictable. Shame. Can you imagine what a fantastic business that would be?"

Jacob felt Clara's eyes on him, but she turned her head away when he looked at her. He still felt her skin under his fingers.

Stop it, Jacob.

"Did you find the entrance?" he asked Fox.

"Yes." She turned her back on him. "It reeks of death."

"Nonsense." Valiant waved his hand dismissively. "It's a natural tunnel that leads to one of their underground roads. Most of them are well guarded these days, but this one's fairly safe."

"Fairly safe?" Jacob could feel the scars on his back. "And how do you know about it?"

Valiant rolled his eyes, despairing of such distrust. "Their King has banned the trade in a number of very popular semiprecious stones. Fortunately, some of his subjects are still as interested as I am in a healthy trade."

"I'm telling you, it smells of death." Fox's voice sounded even more hoarse than usual.

"You're welcome to try the main entrance!" Valiant sneered. "Maybe Jacob Reckless can become the first human to saunter into the King's fortress without ending up cast in amber."

Clara hid her hands behind her back as if she could make them forget whom they'd touched.

Jacob avoided looking at her. He reloaded his pistol and fetched a few things from his saddlebags: the snuffbox, the green glass vial, the looking glass, and Chanute's knife. Then he filled his pockets with bullets.

Fox was sitting under the bushes. As Jacob approached her, she cowered, as she'd done when he first found her caught in the trap.

"Keep a lookout for Goyl patrols," he said. "Better hide the horses between the rocks. And if I'm not back by tomorrow evening, you take her back to the tower."

Her. He didn't even dare say her name.

"I don't want to stay with her."

"Please, Fox."

"You won't come back. Not this time."

She bared her fangs, but she didn't bite. Her bites had always carried love.

"Reckless." The Dwarf poked him impatiently in the back with the butt of his rifle. "I thought you were in a hurry."

Valiant had refashioned the rifle into a rather bizarre weapon. There were rumors that in Dwarf hands, metal could even grow roots.

Jacob got up.

Clara was still standing by the stream. She turned away as he approached, but Jacob pulled her with him. Away from the Dwarf. Away from Fox and her anger.

"Look at me."

She wanted to free herself, but he held on to her, even though it set his heart racing once again.

"It meant nothing, Clara! Nothing!"

Her eyes were dark with shame.

"You love Will. Do you hear me? If you forget that, we can't help him. Nobody can."

She nodded, but in her eyes he saw the same madness he still felt himself. How long would it last?

He took her hands. "You wanted to know what I'm planning to do. I'm going to find the Dark Fairy and get her to give Will his skin back."

He saw the shock in her eyes and put his finger on her lips. "Fox can't know about this," he whispered. "She'll just try to follow me. But I swear to you, I will find her, you will wake Will, and everything will be okay."

He wanted to hold her. He'd never wanted anything so badly. But he let go.

Jacob didn't look back as he followed the Dwarf into the night. And Fox did not come after him.

35. IN THE EARTH'S WOMB

Fox had been right. The cave Valiant led Jacob to smelled of death, and you didn't need a vixen's delicate nose to detect it. Jacob took just one glance inside and knew immediately what creature dwelled there. The floor was littered with bones. Ogres dwelled surrounded by their leftovers and, contrary to popular belief, not only ate humans but also gorged themselves on

Dwarfs and Goyl. Items strewn among the bones hinted at the people who had died here: a pocket watch; the torn sleeve of a dress; a child's shoe, heart-wrenchingly small; a notebook, the writing rendered illegible by dried blood.

Jacob's first instinct was to return and warn Clara, but Valiant made him go on. "Don't worry," he whispered. "The Goyl took care of all the Ogres around here a long time ago. But, lucky for us, they never found this tunnel."

The crack in the rock through which Valiant disappeared was wide enough for a Dwarf, but Jacob had to squeeze himself through it. The tunnel was so low that he could barely walk upright through the first few yards, and soon it descended quite steeply. Jacob had trouble breathing in the confined space and was very relieved when they finally came upon one of the underground roads that connected the Goyl fortresses. It was as wide as a human road and paved with fluorescent stones, which glowed when Valiant shone the flashlight on them. Jacob thought he could hear machines and a constant hum, like the sound of a swarm of wasps in an orchard.

"What is that?" he asked the Dwarf, in a lowered voice.

"Insects. They clean the Goyls' sewage. Goyl cities smell much better than ours." Valiant pulled a pen from his pocket. "Bend down! It's time for your slave mark. P for Prussan," he whispered, drawing the Goyl letter onto Jacob's forehead. "That's your owner's name, should anybody ask you. He's a merchant I do business with. Come to think of it, Prussan's slaves are much cleaner than you, and they definitely don't wear weapons belts. You'd better give that to me."

"No, thanks," Jacob hissed back, buttoning his coat over the belt. "If they stop me, I'd rather not have to rely on you."

The next road they came to was as wide as the grand boulevards of the Empress's capital. This one, however, was lined not with trees but with walls of solid rock. As Valiant pointed the flashlight at them, faces emerged from the darkness. Jacob had always thought it was a myth that the Goyl honored their heroes by cutting off their heads and building them into the walls of their cities. But like all such stories, this one clearly had a grain of very dark truth to it. Staring down at them were hundreds of heads, set side by side, like monstrous flagstones. The faces were, as with all Goyl, unchanged by death, except that the decayed eyes had been replaced with golden topaz.

Valiant didn't stay on the Boulevard of the Dead for long. Instead, he chose tunnels that were narrow, like mountain roads, and that led farther into the depths. More and more often, Jacob saw dim lights at the end of some passage. He felt the activity of machinery like a subtle vibration on his skin. A few times they heard the sound of hooves or wheels approaching, but they always found dark nooks where they could hide in thickets of stalagmites or behind curtains of dripstone.

The sound of dripping water was everywhere, constant and inescapable, and the darkness revealed the miracles it had formed over thousands of years: waterfalls of petrified chalk-white froth, forests of stony needles hanging above them from the ceilings, and crystal flowers blossoming in the dark. In some caves, there was barely a trace of the Goyl—just a straight path leading through the thickets of stone, or a few perfectly square tunnel openings. Other caves had stone facades and mosaics that seemed to originate from earlier times, ruins among the columns that water had grown from the rock.

Jacob felt as if they had been traveling for days through this underground world, when they reached a cave with a lake. The walls were covered with plants that needed no sun, and across the water spanned an endless bridge that was barely more than a stone arch reinforced with steel. Every step rang out treacherously loud through the wide cave and sent clouds of shrieking bats swooping from the ceiling. When the pair had crossed the bridge halfway, Valiant stopped so abruptly that Jacob nearly stumbled over him.

The body that was blocking their path wasn't Goyl; it was human. The sign of the King was tattooed onto his forehead, and his wrists were raw from manacles. There were gaping wounds in his throat and chest.

"A prisoner of war. They use them as slave labor." Valiant stared apprehensively at the cave ceiling.

Jacob drew his pistol. "What killed him?"

The Dwarf let the beam of the flashlight wander over the stalactites above. "The Guardians," he whispered. "The Goyl breed them to defend the outer tunnels and roads. They come out only when they scent something that isn't Goyl. I never had any trouble with them on this route before! Wait!"

The flashlight found a row of worryingly large holes in the cave's ceiling, and Valiant muttered a curse.

A chirping sound cut through the silence—sharp, like a warning cry.

"Run!" The Dwarf leaped over the body, grabbing Jacob's arm and pulling him along. The air was suddenly filled with the flutter of leathery wings. The Guardians of the Goyl dove out from the stalactites like birds of prey, pale and almost humanlike creatures. Their wings tapered into sharp talons. Their eyes were milky and blind, but clearly their ears guided them quite reliably. Jacob shot two in midflight, and Valiant killed one that was digging its claws into Jacob's back, but three more were already crawling out of the holes above them. One tried to swipe the pistol from Jacob's hand, but he slammed his head into the pale face and hacked off one of its wings with his saber. The creature screamed so loudly that he was sure it would alert dozens more of its brethren, but fortunately not all of the holes seemed to be inhabited.

The Guardians were clumsy attackers, but at the

end of the bridge one of them still managed to take Valiant down. The bared fangs were already at the Dwarf's throat when Jacob rammed his saber between the wrinkled wings. Up close it looked like a human embryo, and even the body was childlike. Jacob felt nauseated, as though he'd never killed before.

They escaped into the next tunnel, their arms and shoulders torn, but fortunately none of the wounds were deep, and the Dwarf was too upset to notice the iodine Jacob dripped onto his bleeding hand.

"That gold tree had better last a good long time!" he said, growling as Jacob bandaged his hand. "If not, you just accrued a whole new set of debts."

Two Guardians still circled the bridge, but they didn't follow them into the tunnel.

The exertions of the fight hadn't made breathing any easier, and the maze of dark tunnels seemed end-less. Jacob was just beginning to wonder whether the Dwarf was playing another dirty trick on him, when the tunnel suddenly took a sharp bend, and everything seemed to dissolve into light.

"And here it is!" Valiant said breathlessly. "The lair of the beast, or the lion's den, depending on whose side you happen to be on."

The tunnel had ended high up in a cave that was so

vast Jacob couldn't see where it ended. Countless lamps gave off the kind of dim light Goyl eyes liked best, and they seemed to run not on gas but on electricity. They illuminated a city that looked as if it had been extruded by the rock itself. Houses, towers, and palaces grew from the bottom of the cave and up its walls, like a wasps' nest. Dozens of bridges arched over the expanse of houses, as if there were nothing simpler than elevating iron through the air. The struts grew up like metal stalks from between the roofs. Jacob saw railway lines, streets, and footpaths, all crisscrossing the air above the city. Some of the bridges were lined with buildings, like the medieval bridges of his own world—floating alleyways under a sandstone sky. Higher up, above the houses and the web of bridges that looked as if it had been woven by a steel-spinning spider, hung a series of gigantic stalactites. The largest one was dotted with metal towers pointing downward like spears, and the whole structure glowed as if its walls had been saturated with the moonlight of the world above.

"Is that the palace?" whispered Jacob to the Dwarf. "No wonder they're not impressed by our buildings. And when did they build those bridges?"

"How would I know?" Valiant replied in a low voice. "They don't teach Goyl history at Dwarf schools. The palace is more than seven hundred years old. Their King apparently is planning a more modern version, as he thinks it's too old-fashioned. The other stalactites are military barracks and prisons." The Dwarf gave Jacob a devious smile. "Want me to find out which one your brother's in? Your gold coins will loosen even Goyl tongues. As long as there's a little extra for me."

When Jacob produced two more coins, Valiant couldn't help himself. He stretched, then pushed his short fingers into Jacob's coat pocket.

"Nothing!" he muttered. "Nothing at all. Is it this coat? No, can't be; it also worked with the other coat. Is it something you do with your fingers?"

"Something like that," Jacob answered. He yanked the Dwarf's hand out of his pocket before he could find the handkerchief.

"I'll figure it out one of these days!" the Dwarf grumbled. He tucked the two coins into his velvet waistcoat. "And now keep your head bowed. You're a slave."

The trails that led down along the cave walls were

even more impassable for a human than the streets of Terpevas. Some of the paths were so steep that Jacob's feet kept slipping, and he had to constantly clutch at doorframes and window ledges. Valiant, however, moved through them as quickly as a Goyl. The humans they encountered looked green from lack of sunlight. Most of them had the initials of their owners branded or etched into their foreheads. They didn't acknowledge Jacob, and neither did the Goyl they passed in the gloomy labyrinth of houses. The Dwarf by Jacob's side seemed to be explanation enough, and Valiant relished loading him with all the things he purchased from the various shops at which he inquired about Will's whereabouts.

"Bingo!" he finally whispered, after making Jacob wait for more than half an hour in front of a jeweler's. "Good news and bad news," the Dwarf continued quietly. "The good news is, I found out what we wanted to know. The King's most trusted man brought a prisoner to the fortress, someone the Dark Fairy apparently sent him to find. That's definitely our jasper friend, but it looks as if word hasn't spread yet that the prisoner has a jade skin."

"And what's the bad news?"

"He's in the palace. In the Fairy's quarters. And he's fallen into a deep sleep from which not even the Fairy has managed to wake him. I assume you know what that's about?"

"Yes." Jacob looked up at the large stalactite.

"Forget it!" the Dwarf hissed. "Your brother might as well have dissolved into thin air. The Fairy's chambers are right at the very tip there. You'd have to fight your way through the entire palace. Not even you can be crazy enough to try that."

Jacob studied the dark windows in the shimmering stony facade.

"Can you get an appointment with the officer you do business with?"

"And then what?" Valiant shook his head and sneered. "The slaves in the palace all have the King's mark burnt into their foreheads. Even if your brotherly love extends to doing that to yourself, none of them is allowed to leave the upper parts of the palace."

"What about the bridges?"

"What about them?"

Two of them were directly linked to the palace. One was a railway bridge that vanished into a tunnel in the upper part of the cave. The second was one of the bridges with houses, and it connected to the stalactite halfway down. There were no buildings near where it entered the palace, and Jacob got a clear view of an onyx-black gate and a double line of sentries.

"That expression on your face!" Valiant muttered. "I don't like it at all."

Jacob ignored him. He was looking at the metal trusses that held up the bridge. They looked from a distance as if they had been added later to support an older stone structure, and they stuck like claws into the side of the hanging palace.

Jacob ducked into an entrance and pointed his spyglass at the stalactite. "The windows have no bars," he whispered.

"Why would they?" Valiant whispered back. "Only the birds and the bats can get anywhere near them."

The Dwarf fell silent as a group of children filed past the alley. Jacob had never seen a Goyl child before, and for a moment he thought he recognized his brother in one of the boys. Once they'd passed, Valiant looked back up at the bridge.

"Hold on!" he hissed. "Now I know what you're planning to do! It's insane! Even you aren't that stupid!"

Jacob pushed the spyglass back into his coat. "If you want that gold tree, you'd better get me on that bridge!"

He would find Will. Even though he had kissed his girl.

36. The Wrong Name

"Fox?" There. She was calling her again. Fox fantasized about the Waterman dragging Clara down into his pond, the wolves tearing at her skin, or the Dwarf selling her to the highest bidder at some slave market. The Red Fairy had never made Fox feel that way; neither had the Witch into whose hut Jacob had vanished every night some years ago, nor the Empress's maid

whose sweet flowery perfume she had once smelled on his clothes for weeks.

"Fox? Where are you?"

Shut up!

Fox ducked under the bushes. She couldn't tell anymore whether she was wearing fur or skin. She no longer wanted her fur. She wanted skin, and lips, so he could kiss them as he had kissed Clara's lips. She couldn't stop picturing Clara in his arms, again and again.

Jacob.

What was this yearning, tearing at her insides like hunger and thirst? It couldn't be love. Love was warm and soft, like a bed of leaves. But this was dark, like the shade under a poisonous shrub, and it was hungry. So hungry.

It must have some other name, just as there couldn't be the same word for life and death, or for moon and sun.

Jacob. Even his name suddenly tasted different. And Fox felt a cold breeze on her human skin.

"Fox?" Clara knelt down on the damp moss in front of her.

Her hair was like gold. Fox's hair was always red,

red like the fur of a vixen. She couldn't remember whether it had ever been different.

She shoved Clara away and stood up. It felt good to be the same size as her.

"Fox." Clara reached for her arm as she pushed past her. "I don't even know your name. Your real name, I mean."

Real? What was real about it? And how was it any of her business? Not even Jacob knew her human name. *"Celeste, wash your face. Celeste, comb your hair."*

"Do you still feel it?" Fox stared into her blue eyes. Jacob could look you in the eye and lie. He was very good at it, but not even he could fool the vixen.

Clara averted her gaze, but Fox could smell what she was feeling, all the fear and shame. "Have you ever drunk Larks' Water?"

"No," Fox answered disdainfully. "No vixen would ever be so stupid." Who cared that it was a lie?

Clara stared at the stream. The dead larks were still stuck between the stones. Clara. Her name sounded like glass and cool water, and Fox had liked her so much until Jacob kissed her.

It still stung.

Call back the fur, Fox. But she couldn't. She wanted

to feel her skin, her hands, and the lips that could kiss. Fox turned her back to Clara, fearful that her human face could give her away. She didn't even know anymore what it looked like. She had never cared. Was it pretty? Ugly? Her mother had been pretty, and her father had beaten her nevertheless. Or because of it.

"Why do you prefer being a fox?" The night had tinted Clara's eyes black. "Does it make the world easier to understand?"

"Foxes don't try to understand it."

Clara rubbed her arms as if she could still feel Jacob's hands on them. And Fox could see she wished for a fur of her own.

37. At the Dark Fairy's Windows

Butchers, tailors, bakers, jewelers. The bridge leading to the hanging palace was like a dizzyingly high shopping street. The windows displayed gems and minerals next to lizard meat and the black-leaved cabbage that grew without sunlight. There was bread, and there were fruits from the provinces above the ground, and the dried bugs that were considered a

delicacy by the Goyl. But all Jacob cared about was the palace beyond the storefronts.

It hung from the roof of the cave like a sandstone chandelier. Jacob felt quite dizzy as he leaned over the balustrade between two shops to look down at where the stalactite ended in a crystal crown, with its shimmering points reaching into the void.

"Which are the windows of the Dark Fairy's chambers?"

"The malachite ones." Valiant looked around nervously.

There were a lot of soldiers on the bridge—not just the sentries by the palace gate, but also among the crowds strolling past the shops. Many of the Goyl women wore dresses embroidered with stones that matched the color of their skin. The stones were so finely cut that the fabric glistened like snakeskin, and Jacob caught himself wondering what Clara would look like in such a dress. *How long will this last?*

The Fairy's windows gaped like green eyes from the light sandstone. Barely twenty yards above them was the point where the bridge's metal joists were bolted to the palace wall, but the facade, in contrast to that of the other stalactites, was shiny-smooth and afforded no purchase.

And yet he had to try. Behind him, Valiant was muttering something about the limitations of the human mind. Jacob pulled the snuffbox from his pocket. It contained one of the most usefully magical items he'd ever found: a very long single golden hair. The Dwarf fell silent as Jacob began to rub the hair between his fingers. It began to sprout more fibers, each as fine as the silk of a spider. Soon the hair was as thick as Jacob's middle finger and stronger than any rope in this or the other world. But it wasn't just its strength that made it such a useful tool. It had other, even more wondrous properties. The rope could grow to any length you desired, and it could attach itself to the exact spot you looked at when you threw it.

"A Rapunzel-hair. Not bad!" Valiant murmured as Jacob took the rope and looked down at the green windows. "But not even that rope will help you with the guards. They'll see you as clearly as they'd see a bug crawling over their faces!"

In reply, Jacob produced the green glass bottle from his pocket. He had stolen it from a Stilt, and it was filled with the slime of a snail that could make you invisible for a few hours. The carnivorous snails that produced it used this camouflage to sneak up on any prey they fancied. Stilts and Thumblings bred the snails for the slime, which enabled them to go on their forays similarly undetected. The slime had to be smeared under one's nose—quite an unsavory procedure, even though it didn't smell—and the effect was immediate. The only problems were the side effects, including hours of debilitating nausea as well as, after repeated use, temporary paralysis.

"Rapunzel-hair and waneslime." Jacob heard a trace of admiration in the Dwarf's voice. "I must admit, you're quite well equipped. All the same, I'd just as soon know where your gold tree is before you climb over there."

Jacob was already smearing the slime under his nose.

"Oh no," he said. "What if you've again neglected to tell me something, and the King's guards are waiting for me down there? The rope is strong enough for only one, so you get to stay up here. But if the guards spot me, then you'd better find a way to distract them; otherwise you can say good-bye to your gold tree."

Before the Dwarf could protest, Jacob swung himself over the balustrade. The slime already made his body disappear, as if the darkness were swallowing it up. As he climbed down to the iron girders, he could no longer see his own hands. Holding on to one of the struts, he threw the rope. The golden cord wound through the air like a snake wriggling through water, until it attached itself to a ledge between the malachite windows.

What if you actually find Will behind there, Jacob? Even if you can break the Dark Fairy's spell, he'll still be asleep. How are you going to get him out of the fortress? He didn't know the answer. He just knew that he had to try. And that he could still feel Clara's lips on his own.

Climbing a Rapunzel-rope was easy. The rope adhered to his hands as if it were trying to hold on to them. Jacob tried to ignore the abyss beneath him. *All will be well.* The stalactite inched toward him, sinewy, like a muscle cast in stone. He already felt the nausea brought on by the waneslime. *A few more yards, Jacob. Don't look down. Ignore the height.*

He tightened his grip on the taut rope and climbed on until finally his invisible hands touched the smooth wall. His feet found the ledge and, leaning against the cool stone, he took a moment to recover his breath. The green windows to his left and his right shimmered like hardened water. *What now, Jacob? You can't just break one.* That would have immediately summoned all the guards.

He pulled Chanute's knife from his belt and set the blade against the glass. He noticed the hole with the moonstone rim only after the snake had shot out of it. Moonstone as pale as the snake's scales, as pale as its mistress's skin. It wrapped itself around Jacob's neck before he realized what was happening. He tried to ram the knife through the scales, but it entangled him so relentlessly that his fingers let go of the haft, and he could do nothing but claw in desperation at the scaly body. His feet slipped, and he hung helplessly above the abyss like a snared bird, the strangling snake around his throat. Two more serpents slithered out of another hole next to him and wrapped themselves around his chest and legs. Jacob fought for breath, and the last thing he saw was the golden rope coming away from the ledge with a sudden jolt and disappearing into the darkness above him.

38. FOUND AND LOST

Sandstone walls and iron bars. A lizard-skin boot kicking him in the ribs. Gray uniforms in the red fog that filled his head. At least the snakes were gone, and he could breathe. *The Dwarf sold me out again* was the only thought that penetrated the red fog. *When had he done it, Jacob? In one of the stores, while you were waiting like a sheep?*

He wanted to sit up, but they had bound his hands, and his throat hurt so much that he had trouble swallowing.

"Who brought you back from the dead? Her sister?"

The jasper Goyl stepped out of the dark.

"I didn't believe it when the Fairy told me you were still alive. That was a well-aimed good shot." He spoke the dialect of the Empire with a heavy accent. "It was her idea to spread the word your brother was with her, and you went for it like a fly into the spider's web. Bad luck the snakes aren't even fooled by waneslime. But you did much better than the two onyx Goyl who tried to climb down to the King's chambers. We had to scrape their remains from the roofs of the city."

Jacob pushed his back against the wall and managed to sit up. The cell they had thrown him into was no different from the cells in a human prison. The same metal bars, the same desperate scrawls on the walls.

"Where's my brother?" His voice was so hoarse that he could barely hear himself. And he felt extremely sick from the waneslime.

The Goyl didn't answer.

"Where did you leave the girl?" he asked instead.

He surely didn't mean Fox. What did they want with Clara? *What do you think, Jacob? Your brother is sleeping, and they can't wake him. That's good news, isn't it?* And that Valiant had not given her away proved that the Dwarf really had taken quite a fancy to her.

So you just play dumb, Jacob.

"What girl?"

That answer got him another kick in the stomach, winding him as the snakes had done. The soldier doing the kicking was a woman. Jacob thought he recognized her. Of course. He'd shot her out of her saddle in the valley of the Unicorns. It would've been her pleasure to continue kicking, but the jasper Goyl stopped her.

"Leave him, Nesser," he said. "We won't get anything from him that way."

Jacob had heard about the scorpions.

Almost affectionately, Nesser let the creature crawl over her fingers before placing it on Jacob's chest. It was colorless and barely longer than Jacob's thumb, but its pincers shone like silvery metal.

"There's not much they can do to Goyl skin," said the jasper Goyl as the scorpion crawled under

Jacob's shirt, "but yours is so much softer. So...once again, where's the girl?"

The scorpion dug its pincers into Jacob's chest as if it wanted to eat him alive. Jacob managed not to scream until it plunged its poisonous tail into him. He gasped with pain and fear as the venom poured fire under his skin.

"Where's the girl?"

The She-Goyl placed three more scorpions on his chest, asking the same question, over and over. But Will would sleep as long as he did not tell them anything. Jacob screamed with pain until he lost his voice, wishing he had jade skin himself. He wondered whether the poison would at least burn away the Larks' Water—then he finally lost consciousness.

When Jacob woke up, he had no memory of what, if anything, he'd told them. He was in a different cell. From a narrow window, he could see the hanging palace. His whole body was aflame, as if he had scalded his skin. His weapons belt was gone, as were all the other items he'd had with him, but fortunately they had left him his handkerchief. *Fortunately? And how are a couple of gold coins going to help you now, Jacob?* The Goyl soldiers were infamous for their incorruptibility.

Jacob managed to get to his knees. Metal bars separated his cell from the neighboring one, and what he saw through those bars made him forget his pain.

Will.

He pushed his shoulder against the wall and slowly got to his feet. His brother lay as if dead, but he was breathing. There were still traces of human skin on his forehead. The Red Fairy had kept her promise. She had stopped time.

Footsteps echoed down the dark corridor, and Jacob backed against the bars behind which his brother was sleeping. The jasper Goyl. Hentzau—Jacob now knew his name. He was coming toward their cells with two guards, and when Jacob saw whom they were dragging with them, he wanted to smash his head against the metal bars.

He had told them what they wanted to know.

Clara had a bloody gash on her forehead. Her eyes were wide with fear. *Where's Fox?* Jacob wanted to ask her, but she didn't even notice him. All she could see was his brother.

Hentzau pushed her into Will's cell, and Clara took a step toward him, but then she stopped, as if remembering that only a few hours earlier she'd kissed the other brother.

"Clara."

She turned, her face a torrent of emotions: horror, anxiety, despair—and shame.

She approached the iron bars and touched the red marks on Jacob's throat. "What did they do to you?" she whispered.

"It's nothing. Where is Fox?"

"They caught her, too."

She took his hand as the Goyl snapped to attention in front of the cell. Even Hentzau straightened his shoulders, though his reluctance clearly showed. Jacob knew immediately who that woman was who was coming down the corridor.

The Dark Fairy's hair was lighter than that of her sister; but Jacob didn't wonder how she had earned her name. He felt her darkness like a shadow on his skin, though it wasn't fear that made his heart beat faster.

You don't have to find her anymore, Jacob. She came to you!

Clara shrank away as the Dark Fairy stepped into Will's cell, but Jacob clasped his fingers around the

metal bars that separated him from her. *Come closer!*
Come on! he thought. Just one touch, and the three
syllables her sister had taught him. But the bars put
her as far out of his reach as if she were lying in her
royal lover's bed. Her skin seemed to be made of
pearl, and her beauty surpassed even that of her sister.
She eyed Clara with the same disdain all her kind had
for human women.

"You love him?" The Dark Fairy caressed Will's
sleeping face. "Go on, tell me."

Clara stumbled back, but her own shadow came
alive and wrapped its black fingers around her ankles.

"Answer her, Clara," Jacob said.

"Yes," she stuttered. "Yes, I love him."

Clara's shadow became once again nothing but a
shadow, and the Fairy smiled.

"Good. Then you surely want him to wake up. All
you have to do is kiss him."

Clara cast a pleading glance at Jacob.

No! he wanted to say. *Don't do it!* But his tongue no
longer obeyed him. His lips were numb, as if the Fairy
had sealed them, and he could but watch helplessly as
she took Clara's arm and gently led her to Will's side.

"Look at him!" she said. "If you don't wake him,
he'll just lie like that forever, neither dead nor alive,

until even his soul has turned to dust in his withered body."

Clara wanted to turn away, but the Fairy held her.

"Is that love?" Jacob heard her whisper. "To betray him like that, just because his skin is no longer as soft as yours? Let him go."

Clara lifted her hand and stroked Will's stone face.

The Dark Fairy let go of her arm and stepped back with a smile.

"Put all your love in that kiss!" she said. "You will see; it doesn't die as easily as you think."

And Clara closed her eyes as though she wanted to forget Will's petrified face, and she kissed him.

39. AWOKEN

For a moment Jacob hoped against all reason that the person stirring in the neighboring cell was still his brother. But Clara's face quickly set him straight. She stumbled over the hem of her dress as she backed away, and the look she gave Jacob was so full of despair it even made him forget his own pain.

His brother was gone.

Any trace of human skin had vanished, and he was nothing but breathing stone, his familiar body now cast in jade like a dead insect in amber.

Goyl.

Will didn't see Jacob or Clara as he rose from the sandstone bench on which he had lain. His eyes sought only one face—that of the Fairy. Jacob felt the pain tear through all those protective shells he had fastened around his heart for so many years. It was, once again, just as raw and defenseless as he had last felt it as a child in his father's deserted study, and, as then, there was no comfort, just love. And pain.

"Will?" Clara whispered his brother's name like that of a dead man. She took a step toward him, but the Fairy stepped into her path.

"Let him go," she said.

The guards opened the cell, and the Fairy led Will out.

"Come with me," she said to him. "It's time to wake up. You've slept far too long."

Clara looked after them until they disappeared down the dark corridor. Then she turned to Jacob. Blame, anguish, guilt turned her eyes as dark as the Fairy's. *What have I done?* they asked him. *Why did you not stop me? Didn't you promise to protect him?*

Or maybe he was just reading his own thoughts into her glance.

"Shall we shoot this one?" asked one of the guards, pointing his rifle at Jacob.

Hentzau drew the pistol they had taken from Jacob. He opened the chamber, scrutinizing it like the core of some strange fruit.

"This is an interesting weapon," he said. "Where did you get it?"

Jacob turned his back to him. *Just shoot already,* he thought.

The cell, the Goyl, the hanging palace. Everything around him seemed so unreal. The whole underground city. Fairies, enchanted forests, a vixen who was a girl—nothing but the feverish dreams of a twelve-year-old. He saw himself standing in the doorway of his father's study, Will inquisitively staring past him at the dusty model planes, the old revolvers. And the mirror.

"Turn around." Hentzau's voice was impatient. Their rage was so easily stirred, constantly burning just beneath their stone skin.

Jacob still didn't move. Then he heard the Goyl laugh out loud.

"The same arrogance! Your brother doesn't look like him. That's why I didn't realize right away why your face looks so familiar. The same eyes. The same mouth. But your father never could hide his fear as well as you do."

Jacob turned around. *You're such an idiot, Jacob Reckless.*

"The Goyl have better engineers." How often Jacob had heard that sentence behind the mirror—be it in Schwanstein or uttered by a despairing imperial officer—and he had never thought twice about it.

The father found, the brother lost.

"Where is he?" he asked.

Hentzau raised his eyebrows. "I had hoped you'd tell me. We caught him five years ago in Blenheim. He'd been hired to build a bridge because the towns-people had grown tired of being eaten by the Lorelei. The river has always been swarming with them. It's a lie that the Fairy put them in there. John Reckless. That's what he called himself. Always had a photo-graph of his sons with him. The King had him build us a camera, long before the Empress's scientists came up with anything like that. He built many things for us. Who would've thought that one of his sons would become the Jade Goyl."

Hentzau ran his fingers along the old-fashioned barrel. "He wasn't half as stubborn as you when it came to answering our questions. What he taught us turned out to be very useful in the war. But then he disappeared. I searched for him for months but never found a trace of him. And now I have his sons."

He turned to the guards.

"Keep him alive until I get back from the wedding," he said. "There are a lot of questions I want to ask him."

"And the girl?" The guard who was pointing at Clara had a skin of moonstone as pale as if it had never seen the sun.

"Keep her as well," Hentzau replied. "And the fox girl, too. The two of them will probably loosen his tongue much faster than the scorpions."

Hentzau's steps receded into the darkness. Through the barred windows came the sounds of the underground city. But Jacob was far away, in his father's room, touching the frame of the mirror with a child's hands.

40. THE STRENGTH OF DWARFS

Jacob heard Clara's breathing in the darkness—and her crying. They were still separated by iron bars, but even more by their thoughts of Will. In Jacob's mind, the kisses Clara had given him merged with the kiss that had awoken his brother. And he kept seeing Will opening his eyes and drowning in jade.

He choked on his own despair. The Dark

Fairy had been so close, just a few steps away. Had Miranda watched it in her dreams? Seen how miserably he had failed?

Jacob slammed his manacles against the bars, though all that had gotten him so far were more kicks from the guards.

Clara wiped the tears from her face. How she melted his heart. *It's nothing, Jacob. Nothing but the Larks' Water.*

Through the barred window, the hanging palace shimmered like a forbidden fruit. Will was probably there already....

Clara lifted her head. From outside the window came a scraping sound, a dull grinding, the sound of something climbing up the wall. A hairy face squeezed through the bars of her cell's window.

Valiant's beard was already sprouting as luxuriantly as in the old days, when he'd still worn it with pride. His short fingers easily bent the iron bars apart.

"You're lucky the Goyl haven't had many Dwarf prisoners yet!" he whispered as he climbed through the warped bars. "The Empress has silver added to all bars in her cells."

He dropped down from the window as nimbly as a weasel and took a deep bow in front of Clara.

"What are you looking at?" he said to Jacob. "It really was too funny when the snakes grabbed you. Absolutely priceless."

"I'm sure the Goyl paid you quite well for that show." Jacob got to his feet and quickly checked the corridor, but there were no guards in sight. "And just when did you sell me out? While I spent hours waiting in front of the jeweler's shop? Or was it at the tailor, who supplies the palace?"

Valiant just shook his head while he pulled open Clara's manacles as easily as he'd bent the window bars. "Will you listen to that!" he whispered to Clara. "Can't trust a soul. I told him it was an imbecilic idea to go crawling all over the King's palace like a roach. Did he listen to me? No."

The Dwarf pressed the bars between the two cells open and stood in front of Jacob. "I suppose you're going to blame me for the girls, as well? It wasn't my idea to leave them in the wilderness. And it was definitely not Evenaugh Valiant who told the Goyl where they were."

He leaned over Jacob with a knowing smirk. "They put the scorpions on you, didn't they? Oh, I do admit I would've loved to have seen that."

There were voices from the other cells. Clara

cowered beneath the window, but no one came down the corridor.

"I saw your brother," Valiant whispered to Jacob as he forced open his handcuffs. "If you can still call him that. Every inch of his skin is now Goyl, and he follows the Dark Fairy like a dog. She took him with her to the wedding of her beloved. Half the garrison went. That's why I could risk coming here."

Clara did not take her eyes off the stone bench where Will had lain.

"Up with you, m'lady!" Valiant whispered. He helped her up to the window as though she didn't weigh any more than a child. "There's a rope out there that does almost all the climbing for you, and this building doesn't have any snakes."

"What about Fox?" Jacob hissed.

Valiant pointed to the ceiling. "Right above us."

The facade of the prison stalactite was fissured and craggy, like dripstone, and it offered plenty of footholds, but Clara trembled as she leaned out the window. She held on tight to the balustrade while her feet sought purchase between the stones. Valiant, however, gripped the wall as if he'd been born on it.

"Slowly!" he whispered to her as he grabbed her arm. "Just don't look down."

The Dwarf had rappelled from a narrow bridge barely wider than a footpath. The Rapunzel-rope was stretched taut between the prison wall and the bridge's iron girders, and it was ten steep yards to the bridge.

"Valiant's right!" Jacob said, closing Clara's hands around the rope. "Just look straight up. And stay under the bridge until we come back with Fox."

The golden rope was no more than a spider's thread in the huge cavern. Clara climbed painfully slowly, and Jacob followed her with his eyes until she finally pulled herself onto one of the metal struts of the bridge.

Dwarfs and Goyl were well known for their climbing skills. Jacob, however, had never even liked hiking in the hills, let alone free climbing on the inwardly tapering facade of a building hanging hundreds of feet above a hostile city. But luckily they didn't have to climb far. Valiant had been right. Fox was imprisoned in the cell right above theirs.

She was in her human form, and when Jacob knelt down beside her, she wrapped her arms around him and sobbed like a child. Valiant quickly undid her chains.

"They said they'd skin me if I changed shape!" she sobbed. All her anger was gone.

"It's all right!" Jacob said soothingly, stroking her red hair. "Everything will be all right."

Really, Jacob? How?

Fox, of course, saw the despair on his face.

"You didn't find Will," she whispered.

"I did, but he's gone."

A door slammed farther down the corridor. Valiant cocked his rifle. But the guards were dragging some other prisoner out into the corridor.

Fox climbed as nimbly as the Dwarf. Clara looked very relieved when she and Jacob pulled themselves up onto the iron beam next to her. Valiant swung himself onto the bridge while Jacob rubbed the Rapunzel-rope until it was again nothing more than a golden hair. Some time passed before the Dwarf finally waved them up to the bridge. Beneath them, a platoon of Goyl was marching across one of the lower bridges, and a freight train belched black smoke into the huge cavern as it crossed the abyss. Except for two shafts through which a hint of daylight entered the cave, there was no indication of how the Goyl dealt with their exhaust fumes. *Your father will probably have shown them, Jacob,* he thought as he followed Valiant across the iron planks of the footbridge. But he pushed the thought out of his head. He didn't want to think about his father. He didn't even want to think about Will. He just wanted to go back to the island and forget everything—the Larks' Water, the jade, and the iron bridges that looked as if John Reckless had left his signature all over this world.

"What about horses?" Jacob asked the Dwarf as they ducked into one of the archways that lined the cave's wall.

"Forget it!" Valiant said with a grunt. "The stables are right by the main gate. Too many guards."

"You want to cross the mountains on foot?"

"You've got a better plan?" the Dwarf hissed back.

No, he didn't. And all they had to get past the blind Guardians were Valiant's rifle and the new knife he had brought Jacob—in exchange for another gold sovereign, of course.

Beside him Fox shifted into a vixen again. Clara was leaning against one of the pillars, looking into the depths. She didn't seem to be really with them. Maybe she was back behind the mirror, sitting with Will in the dingy hospital cafeteria. It would be a long journey back, and every mile would remind her that Will was no longer there.

Windows and doors behind curtains of sandstone.

Houses like swallows' nests. Gold-Eyes everywhere. To make themselves less conspicuous, Valiant first went with Clara while Jacob and Fox hid among the houses. Then the Dwarf fetched the others while Clara hid in a dark alley. Coming down the steep roads and stairs was even harder than going up.

Valiant had refreshed the letter on Jacob's forehead, and the Dwarf proudly took Clara's arm, as if he was presenting his new bride to the Goyl. They encountered many soldiers, and every time Jacob pushed past a Goyl uniform, he expected a barked order or a stone hand on his shoulder. But after seemingly endless hours, they finally reached the opening through which they had first looked out over the vast cavern. It was only in the tunnel behind it that their luck ran out.

By now they were so exhausted that they stayed together. Jacob supported Clara, though he couldn't fail to notice the way Fox was looking at him. The first Goyl they encountered were returning from a hunt. There were six of them, and they had a pack of the tame wolves that followed them even into the deepest caves. Two grooms were leading horses loaded with their quarry: three of the large saurians whose spines the Goyl cavalry wore on their helmets, and six bats, whose brains were said to be a Goyl delicacy. They gave Jacob only a cursory glance as they passed by, but the Goyl patrol that suddenly emerged from one of the dark side tunnels was much more curious. There were three soldiers. One of them was an alabaster Goyl—the color of most of their spies.

They exchanged a quick glance when Valiant named the merchant to whom Jacob supposedly belonged. The alabaster Goyl reached for his pistol, calmly informing Valiant that his business partner had been arrested for illegal mineral dealing. Luckily, Valiant was quicker. He shot the Goyl off his horse while Jacob threw his knife into the chest of the second soldier. Valiant had bought the knife in one of the shops on the palace bridge, and its blade cut through the citrine skin like butter. Jacob shuddered as he realized how much he wanted to kill them all. Fox startled the horse of the third soldier, but the Goyl quickly regained control of his mount, and he galloped off before Jacob could pull a gun from one of his dead comrades' belts.

Valiant spat out curses that Jacob had never heard before. While the hoofbeats were still receding, though, they heard a tone that silenced even the Dwarf. It sounded like the chirping of thousands of mechanical crickets. The stone around them sprang to life. Bugs crawled from the fissures and holes; millipedes, spiders, cockroaches, moths, mosquitoes, and dragonflies fluttered into their faces. The creatures landed in their hair, crawled up their clothes, and when they tried to escape into the next tunnel, they were confronted by a solid cloud of fluttering bats.

The alarm of the Goyl had awoken the earth, and it exhaled life—crawling, biting, fluttering life.

They stumbled on, half-blind in the darkness, their arms flailing, creatures crunching under their steps. None of them remembered where they'd come from or in which direction they should be headed. The walls were chittering ever louder, and the beam from the flashlight was a probing finger in the darkness. Jacob thought he could hear hooves in the distance. Voices. They were trapped, caught in an endlessly branching labyrinth, and the fear washed away the despair he had felt in the cells, and reawoke his will to live. To live! Nothing else, just live and get back to the light and the air.

Fox barked. Jacob saw her disappear into a side passage. The hint of a breeze brushed his face as he pulled Clara with him. Light fell onto a wide staircase, and there they were—the very Dragons the ferryman had spoken of. But they were made of metal and wood and were the grown-up brothers of the models that were hanging with dusty wings above the desk in John Reckless's study.

41. WINGS

The alarm could also be heard in the hangar-cave, but at least here nothing was crawling out of the rock, which had been smoothed and sealed. A hint of daylight shone through a wide tunnel. Two unarmed Goyl were standing between the airplanes. They were only mechanics, and they lifted their arms as soon as Valiant pointed his rifle at them.

On their faces, fear of death was written as clearly as their infamous rage. Jacob bound them with a cable Clara found between the planes, but one of them tore himself free and lashed out with his claws. He dropped his hand as soon as Valiant cocked his rifle, but Jacob could only think of the claws that had torn into Will's neck. He'd never enjoyed killing, but the despair he'd felt since Will had followed the Fairy made Jacob afraid of what his own hands might do.

"No," whispered Clara, gently taking the knife from his hand. And for a moment, the fact that she understood the darkness in him bound them even more strongly than the Larks' Water.

Valiant had forgotten about the Goyl. The Dwarf no longer heard or saw anything—neither the chirping in the walls nor the voices coming ever closer through the tunnels. He marveled at the three planes.

"Oh, this is wonderful!" he mumbled, stroking one of the red fuselages with delight. "So much more wonderful than any stinking Dragon. But how do they fly? What do the Goyl use them for?"

"They spit fire," Jacob said. "As Dragons do."

They were biplanes, similar to the ones built in Europe in the early twentieth century. A huge leap into the future, further than anything that was being developed in the factories of Schwanstein or by Her Majesty's engineers. Two of the machines were solo planes, like the ones flown by fighter pilots in World War I; the third one was a replica of a two-seater Junkers J4, a bomber and reconnaissance plane from the same period. Jacob had once built a model of that very plane with his father.

Fox kept her eyes on Jacob as he climbed into the tight cockpit.

"Come down from there!" she called. "Let's try that tunnel. It leads out; I can smell it."

Jacob ran his fingers over the controls, checked the gauges. The Junkers was relatively easy to fly but difficult to maneuver on the ground. *You know this from a book, Jacob, and from playing with model airplanes. You don't seriously think you can fly this thing?* He'd flown a few times with his father, when John Reckless had still escaped his world in a single-engine plane instead of through a mirror. But that was such a long time ago that it seemed as unreal as the fact that he'd once actually had a father.

The alarm was still shrilling through the cave like crickets roused from a freshly mown meadow.

Jacob pumped up the fuel pressure. Where was the ignition?

Valiant looked flabbergasted.

"Hold on! You can fly this thing?"

"Sure!" Jacob managed to sound so casual, he could've even convinced himself.

"How on earth?"

Fox jumped up and barked a warning. The voices from the tunnels grew louder. They were coming.

Clara quickly lifted the Dwarf onto one of the wings. Fox backed away from the plane, but Clara just swooped her up and carried her into the cockpit.

Jacob's fingers found the ignition switch. The engine sputtered to life, and the propeller began to turn. As he made his final checks, Jacob saw his father's hands going through the same motions. In another world. In another life.

"Look at this, Jacob! Aluminum body on a steel frame. Only the rudder is still made of wood." John Reckless had never sounded more passionate than when he spoke about old airplanes. Or weapons.

Fox ducked under the front seat, shivering behind Jacob's legs.

Machines. The sound of metal. Engineered motion. Mechanical magic for those who had neither fur nor wings.

Jacob steered the plane toward the large tunnel. Yes, it certainly was unwieldy on the ground. He could only hope flying it would be easier.

Shots rang out behind them as the plane rolled into the tunnel. The roar of the engine reverberated between the walls. Oil splattered into Jacob's face, and one of the wings nearly grazed the side of the tunnel. *More speed, Jacob.* He accelerated, which made it only harder to keep the wings clear of the tunnel walls, and he took a deep breath as the clumsy plane shot out of the tunnel and onto a graveled runway. Above them, a pale sun was drifting among white clouds. The noise of the engine tore through the silence, and a few crows rose from the nearby trees but, luckily, stayed clear of the propeller.

Pull her up, Jacob! Fox has her fur, your brother has a skin of stone, and now you have a pair of wings.

Engineered magic.

John Reckless had brought metal Dragons through the mirror, and, just like the sheet of paper Jacob had found in one of his father's books, the planes seemed like something else John Reckless had left behind for his elder son.

The plane took off and rose, higher and higher.

Below, Jacob saw roads and railways disappear through massive arches into the mountain. A few years ago, the entrance to the Goyl fortress had been just a natural fissure at the bottom of the mountain. Now jade lizards adorned the arched gates, and the mountainside above them was emblazoned with the coat of arms Kami'en had chosen for himself: a black moth on a shield of carnelian.

The sun drew the plane's silhouette under the moth's wings as Jacob flew past the coat of arms.

He was stealing the King's Dragon, but not even that could give him back his brother.

42. Two Paths

Back. Over the river where the Lorelei lurked, the mountains where Jacob had died, and the plundered land where the beauty was still sleeping in her overgrown castle and where Will had first seen his new kin by the abandoned farm... Within hours, the Junkers covered all the miles that it had taken them more than a week to travel. To Jacob the journey seemed just as

long, for every mile made it more irrevocable that he no longer had a brother.

"Jacob, where's Will?" He'd lost Will many times when they were children, while shopping or out in the park, where he'd felt embarrassed to be seen holding his little brother's hand. As soon as you let go of his stubby fingers, Will would be off stalking a squirrel, a stray dog, or a crow....One time Jacob had searched for hours before he found Will in a shop entrance, his face swollen with tears. But this time there were no more places to look for him, no path he could retrace, no way to undo his mistake, his one moment of carelessness.

Jacob flew south along the railway tracks, hoping they would lead him to Schwanstein. It was bitterly cold in the open cockpit, though he was flying quite close to the ground, and the wind kept grabbing the aluminum-clad wings, forcing him to forget his self-reproach as he fought to keep the wobbling contraption under control. The Dwarf had started to curse behind him every time the plane lurched, even though he probably enjoyed sharing the narrow rear seat with Clara, and Fox uttered an occasional yelp. Only Clara was silent, letting the wind blow away everything that had happened in the past days.

Flying.

It was as though the two worlds had merged, as if there were no longer a mirror. When Dragons turned into machines, what came next?

Such thoughts were not conducive to controlling a biplane, especially not for someone doing it for the first time. The rising steam of a locomotive suddenly robbed his vision, and Jacob pulled up too abruptly. The Junkers tumbled toward the earth as if it had remembered that it wasn't supposed to be in this world. Fox cowered with a whimper, and the Dwarf's curses became louder than the sputtering motor.

Of course, Jacob. How could you have trusted anything your father built?

He felt Clara clawing her hands into his shoulders. What will be his last thought? Will's jade face, or the dead larks?

He didn't get to find out.

A lucky gust of wind cushioned the fall of the groaning plane, and he regained control in time to avoid crashing into the trees. The Junkers pitched like a wounded bird, but Jacob managed to put the wheels onto a muddy ridge. The rudder broke on impact, one of the wings shattered against a tree, and the fuselage was ripped open by the rocky terrain, but finally they came to a halt. The engine died with one last stutter—but they were alive.

Valiant scampered down the remaining wing and immediately vomited beneath a tree. The Dwarf's nose was bleeding, and a branch had grazed Clara's hand, but apart from that everybody was unharmed. Fox was so happy to feel solid ground beneath her paws that she jumped after the first rabbit that stuck its head out of the grass.

Fox cast a relieved glance at Jacob as she noticed the hill with the ruin to their left. They were, in fact, not far from Schwanstein. But Jacob was eyeing the railway tracks running southward to Schwanstein and farther beyond...much farther...all the way to Vena, the Empress's capital city. In his mind's eye, Jacob saw the five bridges, the imperial palace, the towers of the cathedral....

"Reckless! Are you listening?" Valiant was wiping the blood from his nose. "How much farther?"

"What?" Jacob was still looking at the rails.

"To your house? My gold tree?"

Jacob didn't answer. He turned eastward to where the train that had caused their crash was now coming over the hills. White smoke. Black iron.

"Fox." He knelt next to her. Her fur was still disheveled from the wind. "I want you to take Clara back to the ruin. I'll be there in a few days."

She didn't ask him where he was going. Fox looked at him as if she had known this would happen all along. This was how it had always been. Fox knew him better than he knew himself. But Jacob could see that she was tired of worrying about him. And the anger was back. She had not forgiven him for the Larks' Water, nor for not taking her along to the fortress. And now he was leaving her behind again. *Give up!* her eyes said.

You know I can't, Fox.

He stood.

The train grew toward them, devouring the fields and meadows in its path. Fox looked at the locomotive as if its cargo were death itself.

Ten hours to Vena. *And then what, Jacob?* He didn't even know when the wedding was supposed to take place, but he didn't want to think anymore. All his thoughts had turned to jade.

He stumbled down the slope. Valiant shouted something after him, but Jacob didn't look back. The air filled with the smoke and the noise of the train. He broke into a run, his hands gripped metal, his feet found a footboard.

Ten hours. Time to sleep and to forget everything, except for what the Red Fairy had revealed to him about her dark sister.

43. DOG AND WOLF

Trams, carriages, carts, and riders on horseback. Soldiers, workers, beggars, and bourgeois. Maids in starched aprons and Dwarfs being carried through the crowds by their human servants. Jacob had never seen the streets of Vena so crowded. It took him nearly an hour to get from the station to his usual hotel. The rooms had more in common with a Bluebeard's

treasure chamber than with his modest lodgings at Chanute's tavern, but every now and then Jacob liked to indulge himself with the comfort of a four-poster bed. He paid one of the chambermaids to always have a few clothes pressed and ready, which were good enough even for an audience in the palace. The girl didn't miss a beat when he gave her his bloody garments for cleaning. She was used to finding such stains on his clothes.

The bells of the city were chiming midday as Jacob made his way to the palace. On many of the walls he passed, he saw hastily smeared anti-Goyl graffiti competing with the official photographs of the wedding couple captioned with pompous descriptions of the upcoming event. ETERNAL PEACE...HISTORIC EVENT... TWO POWERFUL EMPIRES...OUR PEOPLES...The same obsession with big words on both sides of the mirror.

Jacob himself had once posed for the court photographer. The man was a master of his trade, but the princess could not have been an easy subject. The beauty that Amalie of Austry had gained from the Fairy lily was as cold as porcelain, and her face was as blank in real life as it was on the posters. Her groom, however, photographed like fire turned to stone.

The crowd in front of the palace was so dense that Jacob had to struggle to get through to the wrought-iron gates. The imperial guards pointed their bayonets at him as he approached. Fortunately, Jacob recognized a familiar face under one of the feathered helmets. Justus Kronsberg, scion of an old family of landed gentry. They owed their wealth to the fact that his father's meadows were popular with the Elves whose threads and glass adorned so many dresses at the court.

The Empress required all her guardsmen to be at least six and a half feet tall, and the youngest Kronsberg was no exception. Justus was half a head taller than Jacob, not counting his helmet, but his scraggly mustache couldn't hide the fact that he still had the face of a boy.

Years ago, Jacob had saved one of Justus's brothers from the wrath of a Witch whose daughter he'd rejected, and every year since then their father had sent Jacob enough elven glass to make new buttons for all his clothes, though the rumor that the beautiful glass protected against Stilts and Thumblings had sadly not proved to be true.

"Jacob Reckless!" The youngest Kronsberg spoke with the soft dialect of the countryside around the capital. "Just yesterday someone told me you were killed by the Goyl."

"Really?"

Jacob automatically touched his chest. The imprint of the moth was still on his skin.

"Where did they put the groom?" he asked while Kronsberg opened the gate. "In the north wing?"

The other guards eyed him warily.

"Where else?" Kronsberg lowered his voice. "Are you back from an assignment? I hear the Empress has been offering thirty gold sovereigns for a wishing sack since King Crookback started bragging about owning one."

A wishing sack. Chanute had one. Jacob had helped him steal it from a Stilt. But not even Chanute was ruthless enough to put such an item into the Empress's hands. You just had to name an enemy, and the sack made your foe disappear without a trace. Crookback was rumored to have already dealt with hundreds of men this way.

Jacob looked up at the balcony from which the Empress would present the bride and groom to her subjects the next day.

"No, I'm not here about a wishing sack," he said. "I am delivering a present for the bride. My best to your father and your brother."

Justus Kronsberg was visibly disappointed not to hear more, but he still opened the gate to the external courtyard. After all, it was Jacob's doing that his brother hadn't ended up as a toad at the bottom of some well, or, as Witches tended to prefer these days, as a doormat or a tray for their tea service.

The last time Jacob had been in the palace was three months earlier, when he'd been called to authenticate a magic nut in the Empress's Chambers of Miracles. The wide courtyards now seemed unremarkable compared to what he'd seen in the Goyl fortress, and the buildings surrounding them looked drab, despite their gilded gutters and crystal balconies. The splendor within, however, was still impressive.

The Emperors of Austry had spared no expense, especially in the north wing, for it was built specifically to demonstrate to visitors the wealth and power of the Empire. Golden fruits and flowers twined around the granite columns. The floor was plain white marble (the Goyl were far better at mosaics than any of their neighbors), and the walls were painted with frescoes of Austry's marvels: the highest mountains, the oldest towns, and the most spectacular castles. The ruin that housed the mirror was depicted in all its lost glory, with Schwanstein as a fairy-tale idyll at its feet. No roads or railway tracks scarred the painted hills; instead, they were teeming with all the creatures Her Majesty's family had been hunting with abandon for generations: Giants, Witches, Watermen, Lorelei, Unicorns, and Ogres.

The stairs leading to the upper floors were lined with less peaceful images, commissioned by the Empress's father. Sea, land, summer, and winter campaigns; battles against his brother in Lotharaine, his cousin in Albion, against rebellious Dwarfs, and the Wolf-Lords in the east. Every visitor was sure to find a painting depicting the army of his own nation in battle with the Empire, and of course they were always the defeated. The Goyl were the only ones to have climbed these stairs without having to see their forebears being annihilated in battle. Ever since they had started engaging the humans in war, the Goyl had been the victors.

The two guards coming down the stairs didn't challenge Jacob, even though he was armed, and the servant who scurried past behind them gave Jacob a deferential nod. Everybody in the north wing knew Jacob Reckless, for Therese of Austry often called on his services to give important guests a tour of her Chambers of Miracles and tell them true and untrue stories about the treasures on display there.

The Goyl had been put on the second floor, the most sumptuous part of the north wing. Jacob saw their sentries as he peered down the first corridor. They looked at him, but Jacob pretended not to see them as he turned left from the staircase into a chamber where the Empress demonstrated her interest in the wider world by displaying souvenirs brought back from her family's travels.

The chamber was deserted, just as Jacob had hoped. The Goyl weren't interested in the Troll-fur hat Her Majesty's grandfather had brought back from Yurtland, or in the Leprechaun boots from Albion, and whatever was written about their people in the books that lined the walls was most likely far from flattering.

The north wing was far from the Empress's chambers, thus giving her guests the illusion of being unobserved. But the walls hid a network of secret passages from which every room could be spied on and in some cases even entered. Jacob had used these passageways before, to pay nightly visits to an ambassador's daughter. The network was entered through hidden doors, and one of them was behind a royal souvenir from Lotharaine. The curtain was embroidered with the pearls found in the stomachs of

Thumblings, and the door hidden behind it looked like part of the paneling.

Jacob nearly stumbled over a dead rat as he entered the dark passageway. The Empress had them fumigated regularly, but the rodents loved the dark corridors. Every three yards there were peepholes in the walls, each approximately the size of a thumbnail, which were hidden on the other side by ornamental stucco or behind two-way mirrors. In the first room Jacob checked, he saw a maid dusting the furniture. The second and third rooms had been turned into temporary offices for the Goyl. Jacob instinctively held his breath when he saw Hentzau sitting behind one of the desks. But it wasn't for him that Jacob had come.

The air was musty in the passageways, and the confined space made his heart beat faster. He heard another maid softly humming to herself, the clanking of porcelain—and then a cough, very close. Jacob quickly switched off his flashlight. Of course. Therese of Austry had all her guests watched; why should her greatest enemy be treated differently, even if she was giving him her daughter?

A gas lantern appeared around a corner up ahead, illuminating a pale man who looked as if he spent his entire life in these dark spaces. Jacob squeezed into an alcove, holding his breath until the spy had shuffled past him and out through the hidden door. He was probably going to fetch whoever was relieving him. Jacob wouldn't have much time.

The spy had been watching the very room Jacob was looking for. He recognized the Dark Fairy's voice even before he saw her through the tiny hole. The room was dimly lit by a few candles, and the curtains were all drawn, though a trickle of sunlight seeped underneath the pale yellow brocade. The Fairy was standing by one of the curtains, as though she wanted to shield the King from the light. Her skin shone through the darkness like moonlight made flesh. *Don't look at her, Jacob!*

The King of the Goyl was standing by the door. Fire in the dark. Jacob sensed his impatience even through the wall.

"You're asking me to put my faith in a fairy tale."

Every word filled the room. His voice resonated with power as well as his ability to control it. "I admit it amuses me that those who'd like to see us crawl back into the earth seem to believe in it, but surely you don't expect me to be that naive? No man's skin can guarantee what more than a hundred thousand soldiers have fought for. I am not invincible, and no Jade Goyl will change that. Even this wedding will only buy me peace for a while."

The Fairy tried to reply, but he cut her off.

"We have uprisings in the north; the east is only quiet because they're more interested in slaughtering each other; in the west, Crookback takes my bribes and arms his troops behind my back, not to mention his cousin on the island. The onyx Goyl despise the color of my skin. My munitions factories can't keep up with my trigger-happy soldiers. The field hospitals are overflowing, and the resistance has just blown up two of our most vital railroads. As far as I remember, none of that was mentioned in the fairy tale my mother told me. Let the people believe in Jade Goyl and lucky stones, but these days the world is made of iron."

He put his hand on the door handle and looked at the gold fittings on the door. "They do make beautiful things," he murmured. "I just wonder why they're so obsessed with gold. Silver is so much more beautiful."

"Promise he'll be by your side." The Fairy raised her hand, and all the gold in the dim room turned to silver. "Even when you exchange your vows. Please!"

"He is a Man-Goyl! As far as my officers are concerned, not even the jade can make up for that. And he's less experienced than any of my bodyguards."

"And he still outfought every one of them! Promise me!"

He loved her. Jacob saw it on his face. He loved her so much it scared him.

"I have to go." He turned around, but the door didn't open. "Stop that!" he barked without looking at the Fairy.

She dropped her hand, and the door sprang open.

"Promise me!" she said again. "Please!"

But he left without an answer, and she was alone.

Now, Jacob!

His fingers searched for a hidden door, but they found only wooden panels. The Fairy was walking toward the door through which the King had left. *Come on, Jacob! She's alone now! There'll be guards outside that door.* Maybe he could kick in the wall. And then what? The noise would immediately summon dozens of Goyl, not that she needed them to kill him. Jacob was still in the dark passage, unsure what to do, when one of the guards entered the room.

Jade.

It was the first time he saw his brother in the gray Goyl uniform. Will wore it as though he'd never known anything else. Nothing about him hinted at the human he had once been. His lips might have been a little fuller and his hair a little finer than that of the average Goyl, but his body still spoke their language. He looked at the Fairy as if she were his world.

"I hear you disarmed the King's best bodyguard." She stroked his face, the face her spell had turned to jade.

"He isn't half as good as he thinks he is."

His brother had never sounded like this. Will had never been spoiling for fights or been keen to measure his strength against others'. Not even with his brother...

The Dark Fairy smiled as Will's fingers closed almost tenderly around the hilt of his saber. Stone fingers.

I'll have you pay for him, Jacob thought as his heart drowned in hatred and helpless pain. *Your sister has already set your punishment!*

He'd completely forgotten about the spy. The man's eyes widened as the light of his lantern brought Jacob into view. Jacob smashed his flashlight into the spy's temple and quickly caught the slumping body, but one of the scrawny shoulders brushed against the wall, and his lantern crashed onto the wooden floor before Jacob could catch it.

"What was that?" he heard the Fairy ask.

Jacob extinguished the lantern and held his breath. Steps.

He reached for his pistol, but then he realized who was coming toward the wall.

Will kicked it in as if it were cardboard. Jacob didn't wait for his brother to push through the splintered wood. He was already stumbling back along the dark passageway when the Dark Fairy called the guards.

Stop, Jacob! But nothing had ever frightened him as much as the sound of these footsteps pursuing him. Will could probably see through the blackness as well as Fox—and he was armed.

Get out of the dark, Jacob! He's got the advantage here. Jacob tore down the curtain as he stumbled through the hidden door into the open.

The sudden light blinded Will. He held his arm in front of his face. Jacob quickly struck the saber from his hand.

"Leave the sword where it is, Will!"

Jacob pointed his pistol at him. But Will bent down anyway. Jacob tried to kick the saber from his hand again, but this time Will was quicker. *He will kill you,*

Jacob. Shoot! But he couldn't. It was still the same face, even if it was now cast in jade.

"Will! It's me!"

Will slammed his forehead into Jacob's face. Blood ran from his nose, and he barely managed to deflect the saber before the blade could slash open his chest. Will's next stroke cut into his arm. His brother was fighting like a Goyl, cold and precise, without any fear. *"I hear you disarmed the King's best bodyguard."* "He isn't half as good as he thinks." Another strike. *Fight back, Jacob!*

Blade struck against blade, sharpened metal instead of the toy swords with which they had fought as children. So long ago. Above them the sunlight was caught in the crystal blossoms of a chandelier, and the carpet beneath their feet bore the symbols on which the Witches danced to summon spring. Will was panting. Both of them were breathing so heavily that they noticed the imperial guards only when they cocked their rifles. Will backed away from the white uniforms, and Jacob instinctively stood in front of him, protecting his little brother as he'd always done, but his brother no longer needed his help. The Goyl had also caught up with them. They were coming through the hidden door. Gray uniforms behind them, white ones in front. Will only lowered his sword after one of the Goyl barked an order at him.

Brothers.

"That man tried to enter the King's chambers!"

The officer was an onyx Goyl, and he spoke the language of Austry with barely an accent. Will didn't take his eyes off Jacob as he stepped back to the officer's side. Still the same face, and yet as different from his brother as a wolf was from a dog. Jacob turned his back on him; he could no longer bear to look at him.

"Jacob Reckless." He offered his saber to the guards. "I have come to speak with the Empress."

The guard who took the saber whispered something to his officer. Jacob's portrait, which the Empress had ordered after he brought her the glass slipper, was probably still hanging somewhere in the palace.

Will still had his eyes on him as the guards led Jacob away. *Forget you ever had a brother, Jacob. He already has.*

44. The Empress

It had been a long time since Jacob had last stood in the Empress's audience chamber. Even when he or Chanute delivered something she'd been eager to get for years, it was usually one of her Dwarfs who'd negotiate the reward or give the next assignment. The Empress only granted personal audiences when an item had been particularly dangerous to acquire, as had been the

case with the glass slipper and wishing table, and when the story attached to it had sufficient blood and death in it. Therese of Austry would have made a great treasure hunter if she hadn't been born the daughter of an Emperor.

She was sitting behind her desk when the guards brought Jacob to her. The silk of her bright dress was embroidered with elven glass, and it was as yellow as the roses on her desk. Her beauty was legendary, but war and defeat marked her face. The lines around her brows were more defined, the shadows under her eyes darker, and her gaze had grown even colder.

One of her generals and two of her ministers were standing by the windows through which there was a clear view of the roofs and towers of the city and of the distant mountains the Goyl had already conquered. Jacob turned, and only then did he notice the adjutant standing next to the bust of a previous Emperor. Donnersmarck had accompanied him on three of his expeditions for the Empress. Two of them had been successes and had brought Jacob a lot of money, and Donnersmarck a medal and a promotion. They were friends, though the look Donnersmarck gave Jacob didn't show it. There were a few more medals on his uniform than on their last encounter, and when he walked over to join the general, Jacob noticed that he was dragging one leg. Compared to war, treasure hunting was a harmless pastime.

"Unauthorized entry to the palace. Threatening my guests. One of my spies knocked unconscious." The Empress put down her quill and waved one of her Dwarfs to her side. The servant kept his eyes firmly on Jacob while he pulled back his mistress's chair. The imperial Dwarfs of Austry. Over the centuries, they had thwarted dozens of assassination attempts, two on Therese's father, and the Empress always had at least three of them by her side. Rumor had it they could even take on Giantlings.

Auberon, Therese's favorite among the Dwarfs, smoothed the Empress's dress as she stepped out from behind her desk. She was still as slender as a young girl.

"What is this, Jacob? Did I not order you to find the hourglass? Instead I have to learn that you're in my palace, dueling with my future son-in-law's bodyguard."

Jacob bowed his head. She didn't like it when you looked her in the eyes. "I had no choice. He attacked me, and I defended myself." His arm was still bleeding. His brother's new signature.

"Surrender him, Your Majesty," one of the ministers said. "Or better yet, have him shot yourself, to prove your desire for peace."

"Nonsense," the Empress replied testily. "As if the war hasn't cost me enough already. He's one of my best treasure hunters—even better than Chanute."

She stepped so close to Jacob that he could smell her perfume. There was a rumor that she had magic poppy-juice mixed into it. If you inhaled it too deeply, you did whatever she told you.

"Did someone pay you? Someone who doesn't like this peace? Well, give him a message from me: I don't much like it, either."

"Majesty!" One of the ministers glanced at the door as if the Goyl were listening on the other side.

"Oh, be quiet!" the Empress snapped at him. "I'm already paying for it with my daughter."

Jacob looked at Donnersmarck, but his glance was not returned.

"Nobody paid me," he said. "And it has nothing to do with your peace. I'm here for the Fairy."

The Empress's face went as blank as her daughter's.

"The Fairy?"

She tried valiantly to sound unconcerned, but her voice gave her away. Hatred and disgust—Jacob heard them both. And anger. Anger that she feared the Fairy so much. "What do you want from her?"

"Give me five minutes alone with her. You won't regret it. Or is your daughter happy her groom brought his dark mistress to the wedding?"

Careful, Jacob. But he was too desperate to be careful. She had stolen his brother. And he wanted him back.

The Empress exchanged a glance with the general.

"He's as disrespectful as his former master," she said. "Chanute used that same impertinent tone with my father."

"Five minutes," Jacob repeated. "Her curse cost you your victory. And thousands of your subjects."

She looked at him pensively.

"Majesty!" the general said, but kept his mouth shut after she shot him a warning look. She turned around and returned to her desk.

"You're too late," she said over her shoulder. "I've already signed the treaty. Tell the Goyl he inhaled elven dust or something," she ordered. One of the guards took Jacob's arm. "Take him to the gate, and give orders not to let him in again."

"And, Jacob!" she called as the Dwarfs opened the door. "Forget about the hourglass! I want a wishing sack!"

45. Past Times

Jacob had no idea how he found his way back to the hotel. In every window he passed, he saw his brother's contorted face, and every woman passing him looked like the Dark Fairy.

It couldn't be over. He would find her. At the wedding. At the station, when she'd board the King's onyx-black train. Or in the hanging palace, despite her snakes. He could no longer

tell what was driving him: the hope of somehow getting Will back, the hunger for revenge, or simply his injured pride.

The hall of the hotel was crowded with newly arrived guests, their luggage, and harried bellboys. Everybody had come for the wedding. There were even some Goyl who attracted more looks and whispers than the Empress's youngest sister. She had arrived without her potentate husband from the east and was clad in black fur, as though in mourning over her niece's wedding.

The ceremony would take place the next day, that much Jacob had found out, in the cathedral where Therese of Austry had also been wed, just like her father before her.

The chambermaid had mended and washed Jacob's clothes, and he was holding them under his arm as he unlocked his room. He dropped them as soon as he saw the man standing by the window. But Donnersmarck turned around before Jacob could draw his pistol. His uniform was pristine white, as if to blot out the fact that the more usual colors of a soldier were mud and blood.

"Is there any room to which the adjutant to the Empress does not have access?" Jacob asked as he gathered up his garments and closed the door behind him.

"The secret chamber of a Bluebeard. That's where your talents are more useful than my uniform."

Donnersmarck walked haltingly toward Jacob.

"What's your business with the Dark Fairy?"

They hadn't seen each other for nearly a year, but escaping the clutches of a Bluebeard or searching for the hair of a Devil forges a bond not easily broken. Donnersmarck and Jacob had done that and more together. They'd never found the Devil's hair, but Donnersmarck had kept down the Brown Wolf that had guarded the glass slipper, and Jacob had saved him from being clubbed to death by a cudgel-in-the-sack.

"What happened to your leg?"

Donnersmarck stood in front of him.

"What do you think? There was a war on."

From outside the window came the din of carriages, whinnying horses, and cursing coachmen. Not so different from the other world. But next to Jacob's bed, fluttering above a small bouquet of flowers, were two Elves, barely larger than bumblebees. Many hotels put them in the rooms because their dust helped the guests sleep.

"I am here to ask you a question, and you can probably guess on whose behalf I'm asking."

Donnersmarck brushed a fly off his white tunic.

"If you were to get your five minutes, would the King of the Goyl ever see his lover again?"

It took Jacob a few moments to absorb what he had heard.

"No," he answered. "Never."

Donnersmarck scrutinized him as if he were trying to read from his face what his friend was planning. Finally he pointed at Jacob's neck.

"You're no longer wearing that medallion. Have you made peace with her red sister?"

"I have. And it was she who told me how to bind the dark one."

Donnersmarck adjusted his saber. He had been quite a swordsman, though his leg injury had probably changed that.

"You make peace with one sister only to declare war on the other. It's always like that with peace, isn't it? Always to someone's detriment, already sowing the seed for the next war."

He hobbled to the bed.

"Which just leaves the why. I know you don't care

about this war. So why risk getting killed by the Dark Fairy?"

"The Jade Goyl guarding the King is my brother."

The words seemed to make it even truer.

Donnersmarck rubbed his stiff leg. "I didn't know you had a brother. Come to think of it, there's probably a lot I don't know about you."

He looked at the window. "If it hadn't been for the Fairy, we would have won this war."

No, you wouldn't, Jacob thought. *Because their King is the better general. Because my father showed him how to build better rifles. Because they made the Dwarfs their allies. And because you've been stoking their rage for centuries.*

Donnersmarck knew all that as well, but it was so much easier to blame the Fairy. He struggled to his feet and walked to the window.

"Every evening just after sunset she walks in the palace gardens. Kami'en has them searched beforehand, of course, but his men aren't very thorough. They know there's no one who can harm her."

He turned to Jacob.

"What if nothing can help your brother? What if he stays like them?"

"One of them will soon be married to your Empress's daughter."

Donnersmarck didn't reply to that. There were voices in the corridor. He waited until they'd receded.

"As soon as it gets dark, I will send you two men. They will take you to the gardens."

He hobbled past Jacob. At the door he stopped again. "Did I ever show this to you?" He stroked one of the medals on his chest, a star with the Empress's crest in the center. "They gave me this after we found the glass slipper. After *you* found the glass slipper."

He looked at Jacob.

"I came here in my uniform, and I hope you're aware of what that means. But I call myself your friend, though I know you don't like to use that word. Whatever it is you know about the Dark Fairy, this is suicide. You ran out on her sister and got away with it, but this one is different. She's more dangerous than anything you have ever encountered. Just go and find the hourglass, or the Tree of Life, the Fire Horse, or a Man-Swan. Anything. Send me back to the palace to convey the message that you've changed your mind. Make peace! As we all should."

Jacob saw a warning in his eyes, and a pledge, but still he shook his head.

"I'll be here at dusk."

"Of course you will." Donnersmarck smiled wearily.

And then he was gone.

46. THE DARK SISTER

An hour had passed since sunset, but there were still no footsteps in the corridor. Jacob was beginning to suspect that Donnersmarck was trying to protect him from himself, when he finally heard a knock on his door. There were no imperial guards, however, but a woman.

Jacob barely recognized Fox. She was wearing a black coat over her dress, and her red hair was pinned up.

"Clara wanted to see your brother one last time." Her voice sounded not of brightly lit streets but more of the forest and the fur of the vixen. "She convinced the Dwarf to take her to the wedding tomorrow."

She smoothed her coat. "Looks silly, doesn't it?"

Jacob pulled her into the room and closed the door.

"Why didn't you talk Clara out of it?"

"Why should I?"

He flinched as she touched his injured arm.

"What happened?"

"Nothing."

"Clara says you want to find the Dark Fairy. Jacob?" She took his face between her hands. Such slender hands, still those of a girl. "Is that true?"

Her brown eyes looked straight into his heart. Fox always sensed when he was lying, but this time he had to manage to deceive her, or she would follow him, and Jacob knew he could forgive himself for a lot of things, but not for losing her.

"Yes, I was going to," he said, "but I saw Will. You were right. It's over."

Believe me, Fox. Please.

Another knock. This time it was Donnersmarck's men.

"Jacob Reckless?" The two soldiers standing in the doorway were barely older than Will.

Jacob pulled Fox with him out into the corridor. "I'm getting drunk with Donnersmarck. If you want to go with Clara to the wedding tomorrow, fine, but I am taking the first train back to Schwanstein."

Her eyes went from him to the two soldiers. The Fairy was probably already in the palace gardens.

She didn't believe him; Jacob saw it in her face. How could she? Nobody knew him better, not even he himself. She looked so vulnerable in her human clothes, but she would try to come with him, whatever he said.

Fox didn't say a word as they followed the soldiers to the elevator. She was still upset about the Larks' Water. And now she was about to get even angrier.

"You don't look at all silly in that coat," he said as they waited for the elevator. "You look beautiful. But I still wish you hadn't come.

"She cannot follow me," he said to the soldiers. "I need one of you to stay with her to make sure of that."

Fox tried to shift her shape, but Jacob quickly grabbed her arm. Skin on skin kept the fur at bay. She tried desperately to wriggle free, but Jacob didn't let go. He pressed his room key into the hand of one of the soldiers. Despite his boyish face, he was as broad as a wardrobe. He should be able to keep an eye on her.

"Make sure she doesn't leave the room before the morning," Jacob told him. "And be careful. She's a shape-shifter."

The soldier didn't look too happy about his task, but he nodded and took Fox's arm. The despair in her eyes was painful, but losing her would have hurt much more.

"She will kill you!" Her eyes were drowning in tears and anger.

"Maybe," Jacob replied. "But it won't make it any better if she does the same to you."

The soldier dragged her back to the room. She fought like a vixen, and before they reached the door she nearly broke free.

"Jacob! Don't go!"

He could still hear her voice as the elevator opened into the lobby. For one moment he actually wanted to go back up, just to wipe the anger and fear from her face.

The other soldier was clearly relieved that Jacob hadn't picked him to look after Fox. On their way to the palace, Jacob learned that he came from a village in the south, that he still thought his life as a soldier was exciting, and that he obviously had no idea whom Jacob was hoping to find in the imperial gardens.

The large gate on the rear side of the palace was open to the public only once a year. His guide took forever opening the lock. Jacob once again missed his magic key and all the other items he had lost in the fortress of the Goyl. The soldier chained the gate again as soon as Jacob had slipped past him. Then he took up his position with his back to the gate. Donnersmarck, of course, would want to know whether Jacob ever came out again.

The sounds of the city could be heard in the distance—the horses and carriages, the drunkards, the street vendors, and the calls of the night watchmen— but in the Empress's garden, fountains gurgled peacefully, and from the trees came the songs of the artificial nightingales—which Therese had gotten for her last birthday from one of her sisters. A few of the palace windows still had lights behind them. The stairs and balconies, however, were eerily quiet for the eve of an imperial wedding. Jacob tried not to think about where Will was.

It was a cold night, and his boots left dark prints on the frost-glazed lawn, but the grass absorbed the sound of his steps better than the gravel paths did. Jacob didn't have to look for the Dark Fairy's footprints. He knew where she'd gone. The centerpiece of the imperial gardens was a pond, which was as densely covered with water lilies as the Fairy lake. And here, too, there were willow trees leaning out over the dark water.

The Fairy was standing by the shore, the light of the stars on her hair. The two moons caressed her skin, and Jacob felt his hatred drown in her beauty, but the memory of Will's stone face quickly brought it back.

She spun around as she heard his steps approaching, and he pulled open his black coat, exposing the white shirt beneath, just as her sister had instructed him. *"White as snow. Red as blood. Black as ebony."* One color was missing.

The Dark Fairy swiftly unfastened her hair, but as the moths emerged, Jacob pulled the blade of his knife across his arm. He smeared the blood onto his white shirt, and the moths tumbled down as if he'd singed their wings.

"White, red, and black..." he said, wiping the blade clean on his sleeve. "Snow-White colors. That's what my brother used to call them. He liked that story a lot, but who would've thought they had such power?"

"How do you know about the colors?" The Fairy took a step back.

"Your sister told me."

"She thanks you for abandoning her by telling you our secrets?"

Don't look at her, Jacob. She's too beautiful.

The Fairy slipped off her shoes and walked toward the water. Jacob felt her power as clearly as the cold night air.

"It seems what you did is even harder to forgive," he said.

"Yes, they are still offended because I left them." She laughed quietly. The moths slid back into her hair. "Still, I can't imagine what my sister thought she'd gain by telling you about the three colors. It's not that I need my moths to kill you."

She took a step back. The water of the pond closed over her naked feet. The night began to whir, as if she were turning the air itself into black water.

Jacob could barely breathe.

"I want my brother back."

"Why? I simply made him what he was meant to be." The Fairy brushed her hand through her shimmering hair. "Do you want to know what I think? I think my sister is still too much in love with you to kill you herself. So she sent you to me."

He felt her beauty washing away everything, the hatred that had brought him here, the love for his brother, and himself. *Do not look at her, Jacob!* He clutched his injured arm so that the pain would protect him. The wound caused by his brother's sword. He squeezed it so hard that blood began to run over his hand, and he remembered. Will's face distorted into hatred. His lost brother.

The Dark Fairy stepped toward him.

Yes. Closer.

"Are you really so arrogant as to believe that you could come here and make demands of me?" she said, stopping right in front of him. "Did you really think that just because one Fairy couldn't resist you, we're all doomed to fall for you?"

"No, it's not that," Jacob said.

Her eyes widened as he touched her white arm. The night began to weave a web around his mouth, but Jacob uttered her name before she could silence his tongue.

The Dark Fairy pushed him from her and raised her hands, as though she could still fend off the fatal syllables. But her fingers were already transforming into twigs, and her feet were pushing roots into the soil. Her hair turned to leaves, and her skin to bark, and her cry sounded like the wind rushing through the branches of a willow.

"It is a beautiful name," Jacob said, stepping under the hanging branches. "Such a pity it may only be uttered in your realm. Did you ever tell it to your lover?"

The willow groaned, and its trunk bent over the pond, weeping over its own reflection.

"You gave my brother a skin of stone, and I give you a skin of bark. Sounds like a fair trade, don't you think?" Jacob buttoned his coat over the bloody shirt. "Now I'm going to go and look for Will. And if I find that his skin is still made of jade, I'll come back and set a fire to your roots."

Jacob couldn't tell where the voice was coming from. Maybe it was just in his head, but he heard it as clearly as if she were whispering the words into his ear. "Let me go, and I will give your brother back his skin."

"Your sister told me that you would make promises and that I shouldn't believe you."

"Bring him to me, and I will prove it!"

"Your sister also told me to do this." Jacob reached into the branches and plucked a handful of the silvery-green leaves.

The willow sighed as he wrapped them in his handkerchief.

"I'm supposed to take these leaves to your sister," Jacob said. "But I think I'll keep them to trade for my brother's skin."

The pond was like a silver mirror, and his hand that had touched the Fairy felt burnt.

"I will bring him to you," he said. "Tonight."

A shudder ran through the willow.

"No!" the leaves whispered. "Kami'en needs him! The Jade Goyl must remain by his side until the wedding is over."

"Why?"

"Promise me, or I won't help you."

Jacob could still hear the voice after the pond had long vanished behind the shrubs.

"Promise!"

Again and again.

47. The Chambers of Miracles

"I will bring him to you." But how? For at least an hour, Jacob stood behind the stables that lay between the gardens and the palace, keeping his eyes on the windows of the north wing. There was still light coming from them, candlelight, as the Goyl preferred it. Once he thought he saw the King. Waiting for his lover. On the eve of his wedding.

"Bring him to me."

But how, Jacob?

A children's toy gave him the answer. A dirty ball, lying between the buckets the grooms used to water the horses. *Of course, Jacob, the golden ball!*

He himself had sold it to the Empress three years earlier. One of her most treasured possessions, it was now in the Chambers of Miracles. But no guard would let Jacob back into the palace, and the Goyl had taken his waneslime.

It took him another hour to find one of the snails that produced the slime. The royal gardeners always killed any they could find, but Jacob finally spotted two under the moss-covered ledge of a well. Their shells were already becoming visible again, and their slime worked as soon as he rubbed it under his nose. It wasn't much, but it was enough for a couple of hours.

There was only one guard by the servants' entrance. He was leaning against the wall, and Jacob snuck past him without disturbing his snooze.

The kitchens and laundries were busy even at night, and an overtired maid gave a start as Jacob's invisible elbow brushed her side. Soon he reached the stairs that led away from the servants and up to the masters.

He felt his skin already go numb. He had used the slime only a few days earlier, but fortunately there was no paralysis yet.

The Chambers of Miracles were in the south wing, the newest part of the palace. They occupied six rooms in which all the walls were clad with lapis lazuli, as it was presumed the stone would weaken the magical potency of the artifacts on display. The imperial family always had a penchant for the magical objects of their world, and for generations they'd tried to get their hands on as many of them as they could. It was the Empress's father who had finally decreed that all objects, animals, and humans with magical powers had to be reported to the authorities. It was difficult to rule a world where a pauper could be turned into a lord by a gold tree or where talking animals whispered seditious ideas into the ears of forest laborers.

There were no guards by the gilded doors that the Empress's grandfather had ordered from a smith who'd learned his trade from a Witch. Branches of Witch's birch had been encased within the golden trees that spread their boughs across the door leaf, and whoever attempted to open these doors without knowing their secret would be impaled. The branches would shoot out like lances as soon as someone touched the handles, and like the birches in the Hungry Forest, they aimed straight for the eyes. But Jacob knew how to open the Chambers of Miracles.

He approached the doors without touching the handles. The goldsmith had hidden a woodpecker among the gilded leaves, and the moment Jacob breathed on the golden bird, its plumage became as colorful as the feathers of a living bird. The doors swung open without a sound, as if caught by a sudden gust of wind.

Austry's Chambers of Miracles.

The first hall was filled mainly with magical animals that had fallen prey to various members of the imperial family. Their glass eyes seemed to follow Jacob as he walked past the cabinets that protected their stuffed bodies from dust and moths. A Unicorn. Winged rabbits. A Brown Wolf. Swan-Men. Magic crows. Talking horses. There was also a vixen, of course. She wasn't as gracile as Fox, but Jacob still couldn't bear to look at her.

The second chamber contained Witches' artifacts. The Chambers of Miracles made no distinction between the healers and the cannibals. Knives that had separated human flesh from bone lay right next to the needles that healed wounds with a single stitch and owl feathers that restored the power of sight. There were also two of the brooms on which the healing Witches were able to fly as fast and as high as birds, as well as some gingerbread from the deadly houses of their man-eating sisters.

The cabinets of the third chamber displayed scales from Nymphs and Watermen. These scales enabled whoever put them under the tongue to dive very deep and stay underwater for a long time. There were also Dragon scales in all sizes and colors. Every part of this world had its own stories about surviving Dragons, but Jacob had only once seen a shadow in the sky that looked like the mummified body on display in the fourth chamber. The tail alone took up half a wall, and the gigantic teeth and claws made Jacob actually grateful that the imperial family had eradicated its kind.

The ball he had come for lay on a cushion of black velvet in a cabinet in the fifth chamber. Jacob had found it in the cave of a Waterman, next to the abducted daughter of a baker. The golden ball was barely bigger than a chicken's egg, and the inscription attached to the black velvet sounded just like the fairy tale from the other world: ORIGINALLY THE FAVORITE TOY OF THE YOUNGEST DAUGHTER OF LEOPOLD THE

BENIGN, WITH WHICH SHE FOUND HER BRIDEGROOM (LATER
TO BECOME WENZELSLAUS THE SECOND) AND FREED HIM
FROM THE FROG-CURSE.

But that was not the entire truth. The ball was a
trap that sucked up anyone who caught it and would
release the victim only when its golden surface was
polished.

Jacob broke the lock of the cabinet with his knife.
For a moment he was sorely tempted to also take
some of the other objects, to replenish his chest in
Chanute's tavern, but the Empress would be angry
enough about the ball. Jacob had just tucked it into
his coat pocket, when the gaslights in the first chamber suddenly lit up. His body was already becoming
visible again, and so he quickly hid behind a cabinet
displaying a well-worn seven-league boot made from
the skin of a salamander. Chanute had found the boot
for the father of the Empress. The matching one was
in the King of Albion's Miracle Chamber. Footsteps
echoed through the rooms, and Jacob heard someone getting to work on the cabinets. He couldn't see
who it was, and he didn't dare move, for fear that
his steps would give him away. Whoever it was didn't
stay long; the lights were extinguished, the heavy

doors fell shut, and Jacob was again alone in the darkness.

He was nauseated from the waneslime, but he couldn't resist walking past all the cabinets to check what the other nocturnal visitor had taken. The healing Witch's needle was gone, together with two Dragon claws that supposedly protected from injury, as well as a piece of Waterman skin that was said to have similar properties. Jacob couldn't make any sense of it, but then he told himself that the Empress probably wanted to give the objects to the groom as a wedding present, to make sure he wouldn't be replaced by another Goyl less interested in bargaining for peace.

As the golden doors shut behind Jacob, he was already feeling so sick that he nearly vomited. He was cramping—the first sign of the paralysis caused by the slime—and the palace corridors seemed endless. Jacob decided to follow them back to the gardens. The walls separating them from the street were quite high, but the Rapunzel-rope again did not let him down. At least one useful thing he'd managed to keep.

Donnersmarck's man was still standing by the gate, but he didn't see Jacob sneak away. Jacob's body was still as vague as a ghost, and a night watchman doing his rounds in the dark streets dropped his lantern in fright when Jacob crossed his path.

Fortunately, he was a lot more visible by the time he reached the hotel. Every step was a struggle, and he could no longer move his fingers. He barely managed to reach the elevator, and it was only when he was standing in front of his room that he remembered Fox.

Jacob had to bang on the door so hard that two guests poked their heads out of their rooms before the soldier finally opened up. Jacob stumbled past him into the bathroom and vomited. Fox was nowhere to be seen.

"Where is she?" Jacob asked as he came out of the bathroom. He had to lean against the wall so his knees would not give out.

"I locked her in the wardrobe!" The soldier held up a hand wrapped in a bloody handkerchief like a piece of incriminating evidence. "She bit me!"

Jacob pushed him into the hall. "Tell Donnersmarck that what I promised has been done."

Exhausted, Jacob leaned against the door. One of the Elves that were still fluttering around the room dropped some silvery dust on his shoulder. *Sweet dreams, Jacob.*

Fox was wearing her fur, and she bared her teeth when Jacob opened the wardrobe. Whatever relief she might have felt at seeing him, she hid it quite well.

"Did the Fairy do that?" she simply asked, eyeing his bloodstained shirt. She watched impassively as he struggled to take it off. His fingers were like wood by now.

"I smell waneslime." Fox was licking her fur as if she could still feel where the soldier had tried to grab her.

Jacob sat down on the bed while he still could. His knees were also getting stiff.

"Help me, Fox. I have to go to the wedding tomorrow, and I can barely move."

She looked at him for such a long time that Jacob began to suspect she'd forgotten how to speak.

"A good bite might help," she said finally. "And it would be my pleasure to give one. But first you'll tell me what you're up to."

48. WEDDING PLANS

The first red of dawn reached out across the sky above the city. Therese of Austry had not slept. She had waited, hour after hour, but by the time one of her Dwarfs finally led Donnersmarck into her audience chamber, she'd hidden all the waiting and hoping behind a mask of powder.

"He did it. Kami'en has already called a

search for her, but if Jacob told us the truth, they will not find her."

Donnersmarck didn't look too happy about the news he was delivering. But the Empress's heart beat faster, for this was exactly what she'd been hoping for.

"Good." She touched her tightly coiffed hair. It was turning gray, but she had it dyed golden, like Amalie's. Now she would get to keep her daughter. And her throne. And her pride.

"Give the order."

Donnersmarck lowered his head, as was his habit whenever he disliked one of her commands.

"What?"

"You can kill their King, but their armies are still barely twenty miles away."

"They'll be lost without Kami'en and the Fairy."

"One of the onyx Goyl will replace him."

"And bargain for peace. The onyx Goyl just want to rule underground." She heard the impatience in her own voice. She didn't want to think; she wanted to act. Before her opportunity passed.

"Their underground cities are overflowing. And his subjects will want revenge. They adore their King!"

He was so obstinate, and he was obviously tired of war, but nobody was smarter than him, or less corruptible.

"I won't say it again: Give the order."

She waved to one of her Dwarfs. "Bring my breakfast. I'm hungry."

The Dwarf scuttled away. Donnersmarck still had not moved.

"What about the brother?"

"What about him? He's the King's bodyguard, so I expect that he will die with his King. Did you get those items for my daughter?"

Donnersmarck placed them on the table where she often had sat as a child and watched her father put his seal on treaties and death warrants. Now it was she who wore the signet ring.

A healing needle, a Dragon's claw, and the skin of a Waterman. Therese approached the table and stroked the pale green scales that had once covered the Waterman's hand.

"Have the claw sewn into my daughter's wedding dress," she said to a maid waiting by the door. "And give the needle to the doctor who will be standing by the sacristy."

Donnersmarck handed her the second claw.

"I brought this one for you."

He saluted and turned to leave.

"What about Jacob? Did you have him arrested?"

Donnersmarck stopped short, as if she had thrown a corpse in his path. He turned around, keeping his face as expressionless as hers.

"The soldier who was waiting for him by the gate reported that he didn't come out again. But we couldn't find him in the palace, either."

"You're having his hotel watched, I presume?"

He looked into her eyes, but she could not read his glance.

"Yes. He's not there."

The Empress stroked the Dragon claw in her hand.

"Find him. You know what he's like. You can let him go again as soon as the wedding is over."

"It'll be too late for his brother by then."

"It's already too late. He is a Goyl."

The Dwarf returned with the breakfast. The sun had risen. The night had taken the Dark Fairy with it. Time to claim back what her magic had stolen from her.

Who wants peace when you can have victory?

49. One of Them

Will tried not to listen. He was the King's shadow, and shadows are deaf and dumb. But Hentzau was speaking so loudly that he was hard to ignore.

"With the Fairy gone, I cannot protect you. The additional troops I summoned won't get here before tonight, and the Empress knows that!"

Kami'en buttoned up his jacket. No dress coat for this groom, just the dark gray uniform, his second skin. He had defeated them in it, and he would marry one of them in it. The first Goyl to take a human wife.

"Your Majesty. It's not like her to just vanish like that!" Hentzau's voice betrayed something Will had never heard in it before. Fear.

"On the contrary. It is very much like her." The King let Will hand him his saber. "She hates our custom of having several wives, though I've told her often enough that it also gives her the right to have other husbands."

He fastened the saber to his silver-studded belt and stepped up to the mirror that hung next to the window. The shimmering glass reminded Will of something. But what was it?

"She probably planned this from the start. That's why she had you find the Jade Goyl for me. And if she is right," the King added, looking at Will, "then all I need to be safe is to keep him close by."

"Never leave his side." The Fairy had told him that so often that Will heard the words in his dreams. *"Even if he dismisses you, do not obey him."*

She was so beautiful, but Hentzau despised her. Yet he'd trained Will on her orders, sometimes so hard it had seemed he wanted to kill him. Fortunately, Goyl skin healed fast, and fear had only made Will fight harder. Just yesterday he had managed to strike the saber from Hentzau's hand. "What did I tell you?" the Fairy had whispered in his ear. "You were born to be a guardian angel. Maybe one day I'll grow you a pair of wings."

"But who was I before?" Will had asked.

"Since when does the butterfly ask about the caterpillar?" she'd answered. "He forgets. And revels in what he is."

And yes, he did. Will loved the resilience of his skin and the strength and the tirelessness of his limbs that set the Goyl apart from the Doughskins, though he knew that he'd been made from their flesh. He still blamed himself for letting the one get away who'd snuck into the walls like a rat. Will couldn't forget his face, the gray eyes, goldless eyes, the hair as fine as cobwebs, and the soft skin that betrayed his frailty. Will ran his fingers reassuringly over his own smooth jade skin.

"The truth is, you don't want this peace." The King sounded edgy, and Hentzau bowed his head like an old wolf to the leader of his pack. "You'd rather slaughter them all. Every single one of them. Men, women, children."

"Yes, that's right," Hentzau replied hoarsely. "Because as long as even one of them is alive, they'll want to do the same to us. Postpone the wedding for one day. Until the reinforcements get here."

The King pulled his gloves over his claws. They were made from the leather of the snakes that dwelled deep under the earth, where the heat melted even the skin of the Goyl hunters. The Fairy had told Will about the snakes. She had described it all to him—the avenues of the dead, the sandstone waterfalls, the underground lakes and amethyst meadows. He couldn't wait to see all those wonders with his own eyes.

The King reached for his helmet and brushed the saurian spikes that adorned it. Feathers for the humans, spikes for the Goyl. "You know exactly what they will say. 'The Goyl fears us, now that he can no longer hide behind his lover's skirt. We always knew he only won the war because of her.'"

Hentzau said nothing.

"You see? You know I'm right." The King turned his back on Hentzau. Will quickly lowered his head as the King stepped toward him.

"I was with her when she dreamed of you," he said. "I saw your face in her eyes. How can one dream of something that has not yet happened? Of a man one has never met? Or did she dream you into existence for me? Did she sow all that petrified flesh only to reap you?"

Will's grip tightened around the hilt of his saber. "I think something in us knows the answers, Majesty," he said, "but there are no words for them. I will not disappoint you; that is all I know. And I swear to it."

The King looked at Hentzau.

"Will you listen to that! My jade shadow isn't mute, after all. So you taught him not only to fight?" He smiled at Will. "What did she tell you? That you must stay by my side, even during the vows?"

Will felt Hentzau's milky gaze like hoarfrost on his skin.

"Is that what she told you?" the King repeated.

Will nodded.

"Then that's how it shall be," Kami'en said, turning back to Hentzau. "Have the horses readied. The King of the Goyl is taking a human wife."

50. Beauty and the Beast

A wedding. A daughter in payment, and a white dress to hide all the bloody battlefields. The morning sun made the cathedral windows glow blue, green, red, and golden. Jacob was standing behind one of the garlanded columns, watching as the pews filled with guests. He was wearing the uniform of an imperial guardsman. The soldier he had taken it from was lying

trussed up in an alley behind the cathedral. Nobody noticed the new face; there were so many of them posted all over the massive church, flecks of white in the sea of color that was filling the cathedral. The Goyl, however, looked as though the stones of the cathedral had taken human form. The cool air was probably not to their liking, but the dim light, which not even the thousands of dripping candles could brighten, was ideal for them. Will wouldn't have to hide his eyes behind onyx glasses as he carried out his new duties. *The Jade Goyl. Your brother, Jacob.*

He felt for the golden ball in his pocket. *"Not before the wedding is over."* It would be hard to wait that long. Jacob had hardly slept the past three nights, and his arm hurt from the bite with which Fox had driven the waneslime poison from his veins.

Waiting...

He saw Valiant and Clara come with Fox down the center aisle. The Dwarf had shaved himself again, and not even any of the imperial ministers sitting in the front row were dressed better than he was. Fox looked around. Her face lit up when she spotted Jacob between the columns, but the very next moment the anxiety was back. Fox didn't like his plan, of course. He didn't think much of it himself, but this was his only chance. Once Will followed the King and his bride back into the underground fortress, the Dark Fairy would never get to prove that she could break her own spell.

There was a roar from outside the cathedral, as if the huge crowd on the square had been stirred by the wind.

Finally. They were here.

Goyl, Dwarfs, and humans all turned around to stare at the garlanded portal.

The groom. He took off his black glasses and stood on the threshold. A murmur rose as Will appeared next to him. Carnelian and jade. They seemed made for each other, so much so that Jacob had to remind himself that his brother's face hadn't always been made of stone. Including Will, there were six body-guards who flanked the King. And Hentzau.

The organ on the balcony struck up a wedding march, and the Goyl began to walk toward the altar. Even through their stone skins, they must have felt the wave of hatred surging around them, but the groom looked as relaxed as if he were in his hanging palace and not in the heart of his enemies' capital.

Will passed close enough to Clara and Fox that they could've touched him. Clara's face became rigid with pain, and Fox put an arm around her shoulder.

The groom had just reached the steps in front of the altar when the Empress arrived. Her ivory dress would have done credit even to the bride. The four Dwarfs carrying her train pointedly ignored the groom, but the Empress gave him a benevolent smile before proceeding up the steps and disappearing behind the screen of carved roses that surrounded the royal enclosure to the left of the altar. Therese of Austry had always been a magnificent actress.

The bride would be next.

Once upon a time, there was an Empress who had lost a war. But the Empress had a daughter....

Not even the organ could drown out the roar outside announcing Amalie's arrival. Whatever the crowds on the streets thought about the groom, a royal wedding was still a good occasion to cheer and dream of better times.

The princess wore her Fairy-lily beauty like a mask, but nonetheless Jacob thought he could detect something akin to happiness on those all-too-perfect features. Her eyes fixed on her stony groom as if it had been she, not her mother, who had selected him.

Kami'en awaited her with a smile. Will was still standing right next to him. *"The Jade Goyl must remain by his side until the wedding is over."*

Walk faster, Jacob wanted to shout at the princess. *Get it over with.* Her mother's highest-ranking general, who was leading the bride to the altar, was obviously in no rush.

Jacob looked at the Empress. Four of her guards stood in front of the enclosure and the Dwarfs. And there was also her adjutant. Donnersmarck. He was whispering something into the Empress's ear. They both looked up at the balcony, but Jacob still didn't realize what was going on. *Blind and dumb, Jacob.*

The first shot rang out after the princess had barely walked a dozen steps down the aisle. It came from a sniper hidden next to the organ on the balcony, and it was obviously aimed at the King, but Will pushed him aside in time. The second shot missed Will by less than an inch. The third shot hit Hentzau. And the Dark Fairy was caged in a skin of willow bark in the imperial gardens. *Well done, Jacob. They used you like a trained dog.*

The Empress had obviously kept her assassination plans not only from her daughter. Her ministers were desperately ducking behind the thin wood paneling of their pews. The princess had stopped, and she was looking straight up at her mother. The general leading her tried to pull her away, but both of them were swept along by the screaming guests as they crowded out of the pews. But where could they go? The great doors had been locked. The Empress was obviously hoping to rid herself of a few unwanted subjects as well as the King of the Goyl.

Fox and Clara were nowhere to be seen, and neither was Valiant. Will remained standing in front of his King. The bodyguards had formed a wall of gray uniforms around Kami'en. The other Goyl were trying to fight their way through the crowds to join them, but the imperials shot them down like farmers shooting rabbits in a harvested field.

And you took care of the Fairy for them, Jacob. He pushed his way through to the altar, but one of the imperial Dwarfs immediately jumped him. Jacob elbowed him in the face.

Screams and shots. Silk soaking up blood on the marble flagstones. The imperials were everywhere, but the Goyl stood their ground. Will and the King were still unharmed, though it hardly seemed possible. The Goyl supposedly prepared their skin for battle by exposing it to heat and by eating a plant they bred especially for that purpose. It seemed they had done just that for the wedding. Even Hentzau was back on his feet. But there were at least ten guardsmen for every Goyl.

Jacob gripped the golden ball, but it was impossible to get a clear throw. Will was surrounded by imperials, and Jacob could barely lift his arm without one of the soldiers stumbling into him. They were lost. All of them. Will. Clara. Fox.

Another Goyl fell, then Hentzau went down, and Will was the last man shielding the King. Two imperials attacked the Goyl. Will killed them both, though one of them rammed his saber deep into Will's shoulder. *"Kami'en needs him!"* The Fairy had known. The Jade Goyl, her lover's shield. His brother.

Will's uniform was soaked with the blood of Goyl and humans. The King and he were fighting back-to-back, but they were already surrounded by white uniforms. Soon not even their Goyl skins would save them.

Do something, Jacob. Anything!

Jacob saw a flash of red fur between the benches, and Valiant standing protectively in front of a crouched figure. Clara. He couldn't tell whether she was still alive. Right next to them, a Goyl was fighting four imperials. And the Empress was sitting behind her carved roses, waiting for the death of her enemy.

Jacob fought his way up the steps to the enclosure. Donnersmarck was still standing next to the Empress. Their eyes met. *I warned you*, his said.

Will was fighting three imperials at once. Blood was running down his face. Pale Goyl blood.

Do something, Jacob.

An imperial soldier knocked his arm as he reached for his handkerchief. The willow leaves scattered onto one of the many fallen bodies. Goyl and humans. *Whose side are you on, Jacob?* But he could no longer think of sides, just of his brother, and of Clara and Fox. He managed to snatch up a few of the leaves, and he screamed the name of the Dark Fairy into the roar of the battle.

The bark was still peeling from her arms as she suddenly appeared in front of the altar steps, her long hair covered in willow leaves. She lifted her hands, and glass tendrils grew up around the King and Will, deflecting the sword blades and bullets as if they were children's toys. Jacob saw his brother collapse, saw the King catch him in his arms. The Dark Fairy, however, began to grow like a flame fanned by the wind, and the moths swarmed from her hair, thousands of black insects, latching on to the flesh of humans and Dwarfs wherever they could find it.

The Empress tried to flee, but her Dwarfs and her guards were already collapsing under the onslaught of the moths, and then they also found her skin.

Human skin. Fox was wearing her fur, but where was Clara?

Jacob leaped over the dead and the wounded, whose screams and groaning filled the cathedral. He reached the bottom of the altar steps. Fox was standing over Clara's slumped body, desperately snapping at the moths. Valiant was lying next to them.

The Fairy was still blazing. Jacob tightened his fist even harder around the leaves and stumbled past her. She turned toward him as if she could feel the pressure of his fingers on her skin.

"Call them back!" he screamed, dropping to his knees next to Clara and Valiant.

The Dwarf was still moving, but Clara was as pale as death. White, red, black. Jacob brushed the moths off Clara's skin and dropped the willow leaves to unbutton his white guardsman's tunic. There was enough blood on it, but where could he get something black?

The moths were converging on him as he put his jacket over Clara. With a final effort he pulled a black cravat from a dead man's neck and wrapped it around her arm. Fluttering wings. Stings cutting into his flesh like splinters. They sowed a numbness that tasted of death. Jacob collapsed next to the Dwarf. He felt paws pushing into his chest.

"Fox!" He barely managed to utter her name. She swiped the moths from his face, but they were too many.

"White. Red. Black," he muttered, but she of course didn't understand what he meant. The leaves… he felt around the floor for them, but his fingers were as heavy as lead.

"Enough!"

Just one word, but it came from the only person whom the Dark Fairy still heard in her rage. The King's voice made the moths whirl up. Even the venom in Jacob's veins seemed to dissolve, until only a deep weariness remained.

Valiant rolled over with a groan, but Clara wasn't moving. She didn't open her eyes until Jacob leaned over her. He quickly turned his head so she wouldn't see how relieved he was. However, Clara's eyes sought only his brother.

Will was back on his feet, standing behind the Fairy's glassy tendrils. They turned to water as soon as the King stepped toward them, spilling down the stairs and cleansing the blood from the altar.

The moths landed on the Goyl dead and the wounded, and many of them began to stir. The Dark Fairy embraced her lover, wiping the pale blood from his face.

Will dragged the Empress to her feet and knocked out one of her Dwarfs who tried to stand in his way. Three of the other Goyl were driving the survivors from the pews. Jacob looked around for the willow leaves, but one of the Goyl dragged him up and pushed him and Clara toward the altar steps. Fox hurried after them. Her fur was still the best protection. Valiant was upright again, too. And from behind a distant pew, a slender figure rose. White silk speckled with blood, and above it a dollface that, despite the fear, still looked like a mask.

The princess stepped unsteadily into the aisle. Her veil was torn. She gathered up her dress to climb over the body of the general who had led her into the church. Her long train was heavy with blood.

Her groom looked at her as if he was weighing whether to kill her himself or to leave that pleasure to the Fairy. The rage of the Goyl. In their King, it had turned to cold fire.

"Get me one of their priests," he ordered Will. "One of them must still be alive."

The Empress looked at him incredulously. She could barely stand, but one of her Dwarfs lurched to her side and propped her up.

"Yes?" Kami'en said, stepping toward her, his saber in his hand. "So you tried to have me killed. I don't see how that changes our arrangement."

He looked down at the princess, who was standing at the bottom of the altar.

"No," she answered for her mother, in a halting voice. "It changes nothing. But the price is still peace."

Her mother started to protest, but one glance from the King silenced her.

"Peace," he repeated. He looked at the dead Goyl the moths had not brought back to life. "I think I have forgotten what that means. You shall have your own life and that of your mother as your wedding gift."

The priest Will dragged out from the sacristy stumbled over the corpses. The Dark Fairy's face was whiter than the bride's dress as the princess climbed the steps to the altar. And Kami'en, King of the Goyl, wed Amalie, princess of Austry.

51. BRING HIM TO ME

When Amalie of Austry stepped out of the
cathedral, her dress was covered in flowers. The
Fairy had made white roses from the blood of
the Goyl and red ones from that of the humans.
She had turned the stains on the bridegroom's
uniform into rubies and moonstones, and the
waiting crowd cheered. Some of the onlookers
may have wondered why so few of the wedding

guests followed the happy couple, and some may even have noticed the fear on the faces of the remaining guests, but the noise on the streets had drowned out the shots from the cathedral, the dead were silent, and the King of the Goyl and his human bride climbed into the golden carriage that had long ago taken Amalie's great-grandmother to her own wedding.

An endless parade of coaches and carriages was waiting in front of the cathedral. The Fairy remained at the top of the steps, like a threat, while the surviving Goyl formed a cordon from which there would be no escape. Not one of the imperial soldiers managing the crowds noticed that the carriages were being filled with hostages and that one of them was their Empress.

She was shaking as Donnersmarck helped her into the carriage. He'd survived the carnage, together with two of her Dwarfs. One of them was Auberon, her favorite. His bearded face was swollen from the stings of the moths. Jacob knew only too well how the Dwarf felt. He was numb himself. Clara wasn't looking any better, and Valiant tripped over his own feet as they descended the steps of the cathedral. Jacob was carrying Fox in his arms so that the Goyl wouldn't chase her away. They were all hostages, human decoration, a camouflaged escort for the Fairy's lover, whose troops were standing by barely a day's march away.

What have you done, Jacob?

He had protected his brother. And Will was alive. His skin was jade, but he lived. Jacob only regretted that he had lost the willow leaves and, with them, any hope of protecting them from the Fairy. She watched him as he followed Clara and Fox into the carriage. Her anger still burned on Jacob's skin. He had gambled everything on keeping his brother alive, and in the process he'd turned the Empress and with her half of the Mirrorworld into his enemies.

Each coachman was joined by a Goyl before setting off, and as soon as the carriages reached one of the bridges leading out of the city, the drivers were summarily shoved off their boxes. The guards escorting the wedding couple tried to intervene, but the Dark Fairy unleashed her moths, and the Goyl steered the carriages unimpeded across the bridge, and from there into one of the streets on the other side.

A dozen carriages. Forty soldiers. A Fairy protecting the man she loved. A princess who had said "I do" among the dead. And a King who had trusted his enemies and would surely take revenge for their betrayal.

As they rattled along the cobbled streets, Jacob kept repeating to himself: *Your brother is alive, Jacob. Nothing else matters.* All the while, Valiant was cursing himself for wanting to go to a royal wedding.

Dark clouds drifted across the sky like bad omens as the convoy rumbled through a gate, behind which a group of plain buildings surrounded a wide courtyard. Everyone in Vena knew about the old munitions factory—enough to avoid it. The factory had been abandoned after the river flooded the area a few years earlier, leaving the buildings filled with water and foul-smelling mud. During the last cholera epidemic, the sick had been brought there to die. Not that the Goyl would have been bothered by that. They were immune to most human diseases.

"What are they going to do with us?" Clara whispered as their carriage stopped next to the redbrick wall.

"I don't know," Jacob answered.

Valiant, however, clambered onto the seat and peered out into the deserted yard. "I think I might," he muttered.

Will climbed out of the golden carriage first, followed by the King and his bride. The Goyl pulled their hostages from the other carriages. One of them shoved the Empress back as she tried to reach her daughter, and Donnersmarck quickly drew her to his side.

The Dark Fairy stood alone in the middle of the yard, looking around vigilantly. She was not about to let her beloved stumble into another ambush. Five moths fluttered up from her dress and into the crumbling buildings. Silent spies. Winged death.

The Goyl looked at their King. Forty soldiers who had all narrowly escaped death and were now isolated in the heart of their enemies' territory. *What now?* their faces asked. They struggled to hide their fear under their helpless rage. Kami'en waved three of them to him. They had the alabaster skin of Goyl spies.

"Make sure the tunnel is safe." The King's voice sounded relaxed. If he was afraid, he managed to hide it better than his soldiers.

"I bet you my gold tree I know where they're trying to go," Valiant whispered as the three alabaster Goyl vanished between the buildings. "One of our more dim-witted ministers built a tunnel from here to Vena some years ago because he didn't believe there was a future in trains. The tunnel was to supply this factory. I did hear rumors that the Goyl connected it with their western fortress and that their spies like to use it."

A tunnel. *Back underground, Jacob.* If they didn't shoot their hostages first.

The Goyl were herding the prisoners together. Jacob leaned down to grab Fox before she could get lost between all those shuffling feet, but one of the Goyl pulled him roughly out of the crowd. Jasper and amethyst. Nesser. Jacob remembered all too well how she had put the scorpions on his chest. Fox wanted to jump after him, but Clara quickly lifted the vixen into her arms as the She-Goyl cocked her pistol.

"Hentzau's more dead than alive!" she hissed at Jacob as she led him away. "Why are you still breathing?"

She shoved him across the courtyard, past the King, who was standing with Will by the carriages and was conferring with the two Goyl officers who had survived the carnage. They did not have much time. By now someone had surely found the dead in the cathedral.

The Dark Fairy was standing at the bottom of a flight of steps that led down to the river. The stone arm of a jetty reached out into the water, which the refuse of the city covered like a grimy skin, but the Fairy was looking across the river as if she could see the lilies among which she had been born. *She's going to kill you, Jacob.*

"Leave me alone with him, Nesser," she said.

The She-Goyl hesitated, but then she left, giving Jacob one last scathing look.

The Fairy rubbed her white arms. Jacob saw traces of bark on her wrist. "You gambled everything, and you lost."

"My brother is the one who lost."

He was so tired. How was she going to kill him? With her moths? With some curse?

The Fairy looked up at Will. More than ever, he and the King seemed to belong together.

"He was everything I hoped for," she said. "Look at him. All that petrified flesh, sown just for him."

She brushed some bark off her arm.

"I will give him back to you," she said. "But I have one condition: that you take him away from here, far, far away. So far that I won't be able to find him. For if I do, I will kill him."

He was dreaming. Yes. He must be. Some kind of fevered hallucination. He was probably still lying in the cathedral, her moths pumping their venom into his skin.

"Why?" He barely even managed to say that one word.

Why are you asking her, Jacob? Do you really want to

know if this is a dream? If it is, it's a good one. She's giv-
ing you your brother back.

The Fairy didn't answer him anyway.

"Take him to the building by the gate, and wait for me there. But hurry, and watch out for Kami'en. He won't appreciate losing his jade shadow."

Jasper, onyx, moonstone. Jacob cursed his human skin as he crossed the courtyard, keeping his head down. Most of the surviving Goyl were probably not aware that they owed their escape to him. Fortunately, most of them were guarding the hostages or looking after the wounded, so Jacob managed to reach the carriages unchallenged.

The King was standing with his officers. The alabaster Goyl had not returned. The princess approached her husband and talked to him. Finally Kami'en led her away. Will's eyes stayed on his King, but he did not follow.

Now, Jacob.

Will's hand went for his saber as soon as Jacob appeared from between the carriages.

Do you want to play catch, Will?

His brother shoved a couple of Goyl out of his way, and he began to run. His wounds didn't seem to impede him. *Not too fast, Jacob. Let him come closer, just as you used to when you were kids.* Back behind the carriages, past the shed where they'd locked up the hostages, and on to the building by the gate. Jacob kicked open the door. A dark hallway with boarded-up windows. The patches of light on the grimy floor looked like puddles of milk. The next room was full of beds for the cholera victims. Jacob squeezed himself behind the open door.

Will spun around when Jacob slammed the door shut behind him. For a moment his face showed the same surprise as when Jacob had hidden behind a tree in the park, but nothing in his eyes indicated that he recognized Jacob. The stranger with his brother's face. But he did catch the golden ball. Hands have their own memory. *Will, catch!* The ball swallowed him up like a frog swallowing a fly. Outside, the stone King was looking in vain for his jade shadow.

Jacob picked up the ball and sat on one of the beds. His reflection stared back at him from the gold, distorted, like in his father's mirror. He wasn't sure what made him think of Clara; maybe it was the hospital smell that still lingered in the old walls, so different from and yet so like that of the other world. Whatever it was, he caught himself imagining for a moment, just one short moment, how it would be if he simply forgot about the golden ball and put it into his chest in Chanute's tavern.

What's wrong with you, Jacob? Is it the Larks' Water still? Or is it that you're afraid that even if the Fairy keeps her promise, your brother will forever be that stranger whose face is disfigured by his hatred of you?

The Fairy appeared so suddenly in the doorway, as if he'd summoned her with his thoughts.

"Well, look at that!" she said, seeing the golden ball in his hands. "I knew the girl who once played with that ball. A long time before you and your brother were born. She caught not only her husband with it but also her older sister, and wouldn't let her out for ten years."

She walked toward Jacob, her dress wiping over the dirty floor.

He hesitated, but at last he gave her the ball.

"Such a pity," she said, lifting it to her lips. "Your brother looks so much better in jade." She breathed on the gleaming surface until the gold misted over. Then she handed the ball back to Jacob.

"What?" she said, noticing Jacob's doubtful look. "You're trusting the wrong Fairy."

She came so close to him that he could feel her breath on his face.

"My sister didn't tell you that any man who utters my name will die. Death will approach slowly, as befits the revenge of an immortal. You have maybe a year left, but it won't be long before you feel its presence. I'll show you."

She put her hand on his chest. Jacob felt a piercing pain in his heart. Blood seeped through his shirt, and when he tore it open he saw that the moth above his heart had come to life. Jacob grabbed its swollen body, but its claws were sunk so deep into his flesh that it felt as if he were tearing out his own heart.

"They say that to humans, love often feels like death," the Fairy said. "Is that true?"

She crushed the moth on Jacob's chest, until all that remained was the imprint on his skin.

"Release your brother as soon as the gold is clear again," the Fairy said. "There's a carriage waiting by the gate, for you and those who came with you. But remember what I told you. Take him as far away from me as you can."

52. Happily Ever After

The tower, the scorched walls, and the fresh wolf tracks—it was as if they'd only just left, but the wheels of the carriage crunched through freshly fallen snow as Jacob reined in the horses.

Fox jumped out and licked the cold white powder from her paws. Jacob climbed down from the driver's box. He took the golden ball from his pocket. The surface was almost clear,

and it reflected the cloudy morning sky. During their journey, Jacob had looked at the ball so often that Fox had probably guessed what it contained. But he hadn't said anything to Clara yet.

It had taken them two days to get back to the ruin. At the last coach station, the stableboy had told them that the Goyl had turned their King's wedding into a massacre and had kidnapped the Empress, but nobody knew any more.

Fox wallowed in the snow as if she wanted to wash the past days from her fur. Clara looked up at the tower. Her breath clung to her mouth in white clouds, and she was shivering in the dress Valiant had bought her for the wedding. The blue silk was torn and dirty, but her face still reminded Jacob of damp feathers, even though all he saw on it was her yearning for his brother.

"A ruin?" Valiant climbed out of the carriage and surveyed his surroundings with dismay. "What is this?" he hissed at Jacob. "Where's my tree?"

A Heinzel scampered out of the shadows and quickly picked a few acorns out of the snow.

"Fox, show him the tree."

Valiant marched after the vixen so eagerly that he

nearly fell over his own boots. Clara didn't even look at them.

It seemed such a long time since he'd first seen her standing between the blackened pillars. Jacob went over to her.

"You want me to go back, don't you?" She looked at him as only she could. "You can tell me. I'm never going to see Will again. It's okay. You tried everything."

Jacob took her hand and put the ball into it.

The gold gleamed as if it had been cast from the sun itself. *"You're trusting the wrong Fairy."*

"You have to polish it," he said. "Until you can see yourself in it as clearly as in a mirror."

Then he left her alone and entered the crumbling ruin. Will would want to see Clara's face first. *And they lived happily ever after.* Unless the Dark Fairy had deceived him, as her sister had.

Jacob pushed aside the ivy that covered the entrance to the tower. He looked up at the sooty walls and remembered how he had climbed down for the very first time on a rope he'd found in his father's study. Where else?

The skin over his heart was still sore, and he felt the

imprint of the moth like a brand under his shirt. *You paid the price, Jacob, but what did you get in exchange?*

He heard Clara's suppressed cry.

And then another voice spoke her name.

Will's voice hadn't sounded so soft in a long time.

Jacob heard whispers. Laughter.

He leaned against the wall, which was black with soot and damp with the cold caught between its stones.

It was over. This Fairy had kept her promise. Jacob knew it even before he pushed through the ivy again, before he saw Will standing next to Clara. The stone was gone, and his brother's eyes were blue, only blue.

Go, Jacob!

Will let go of Clara's hand. He looked at him, stunned, as Jacob stepped out from between the walls, but there was no rage on his brother's face, no hatred. The jade-skinned stranger had disappeared, though Will was still wearing the gray uniform.

He went up to Jacob, his eyes fixed on his chest as if he could still see the blood gushing out after the Goyl's bullet hit him, and then he hugged him, clutching him as hard as he used to when they were children.

"I thought you were dead. And I knew it couldn't be true."

Will.

He stepped back and looked at Jacob as if to make sure there was nothing missing.

"How did you do it?" He pushed back the gray sleeve and touched his soft skin. "It's gone!"

He turned to Clara. "I told you Jacob would figure it out. I don't know how, but he always could."

"I know." She smiled, and in her eyes Jacob saw everything that had happened.

Will touched his shoulder where the saber had cut the fabric. Did he know that the stains were his own blood? No. How could he? It was pale Goyl blood.

He had his brother back.

"Tell me everything." Will took Clara's hand.

"That's a long story," Jacob replied. And he would never tell it to him.

Once upon a time, there was a boy who set out to learn the meaning of fear.

For a moment Jacob thought he could see a trace of gold in his brother's eyes, but that was probably just the pupils catching the morning sun.

"Take him away. Far away."

"Look at this! I'm richer than the Empress! What am I saying? Richer than the King of Albion!" Gilded hair, gilded shoulders—even Jacob had trouble recognizing Valiant. The gold stuck to him like the sticky, foul-smelling sap the tree had always discharged over Jacob.

The Dwarf pranced past Will without even noticing him.

"I have to admit it," he shrieked at Jacob. "I was sure you'd cheat me. But for this I'd even take you back into the Goyl fortress. Do you think it'll harm the tree if I dig it up?"

Fox also had a few flakes of gold in her fur. She stopped dead when she saw Will.

What do you say, Fox? Does he still smell like them?

Will picked up a small clump of gold that the Dwarf had brushed from his hair.

Valiant still hadn't noticed him. He noticed nothing.

"I'll have to take the risk!" he panted. "For all I know, you might just shake all the gold out of it if I leave it here. No, there's only one thing to do."

He nearly fell over Fox as he ran off again. Will just

stood there, wiping the snow from the tiny nugget in his hand.

Take him away. Very far, so I can't find him.

Clara exchanged a worried look with Jacob.

"Come on, Will," she said. "Let's go home." She reached for his hand, but Will rubbed his arm as if he could once again feel the jade growing on his skin.

Take him away, Jacob.

"Clara's right, Will," he said, taking his brother's arm. "Come on." And Will followed him, although he turned his head once more, looking back as if he had lost something.

Fox followed them to the tower, but she stopped in front of the entrance.

"I'll be back soon!" Jacob said to her as Clara and Will stroked her fur in farewell. "Make sure the Dwarf collects his gold before the ravens get here."

Magic gold attracted Gold-Ravens, and their cawing could drive you insane. Fox nodded, but she hesitated before she turned, and the concerned look she cast was for Clara, not Will. She still hadn't forgotten the Larks' Water. When would he forget? *When they are gone, Jacob.*

He climbed up the rope ladder first. On the floor of the tower room, between some acorn shells, lay a dead Heinzel. The Stilt had probably killed it. Jacob pushed the tiny body under a few leaves before helping Clara through the hatch.

The mirror caught them all in its glass, but it was Will who stood in front of it and gazed at himself as though he were seeing a stranger. Clara walked up beside him and took his hand. Jacob, however, retreated until the dark glass could no longer find him. Will turned to him, a question in his eyes.

"You're not coming with us?"

Not everything was forgotten. Jacob could see it on Will's face. But he had his brother back, maybe more than ever.

"No." He shook his head. "I can't very well leave Fox, can I?"

Will looked at him. What did he see? A dark corridor? A saber in his hand?

"Do you know when you'll be coming back again?"

Jacob smiled.

Just go, Will.

Far away, so I can't find him.

But Will left Clara standing and went to him.

"Thank you, brother," he whispered, embracing him.

Then he turned, and stopped once more.

"Did you ever find him?" he asked.

Jacob thought he could again feel Hentzau's golden eyes finding his father's face in his.

"No," he answered. "Never."

Will nodded and Clara took his hand, but it was Jacob she looked at as his brother pressed his hand onto the glass.

And then they were gone, and Jacob saw just himself in the warped glass.

Fox was waiting where he had left her.

"What was the price?" she asked as she followed him to the carriage.

"The price for what?"

Jacob unhitched the horses. He would take them to Chanute, as compensation for the packhorse he'd lost. He could only hope that the Goyl would treat his mare well.

"What was the price for your brother?" Fox shifted her shape.

She was wearing her own dress again. It suited her so much better than the dress she had worn in the city.

"Don't worry about it. It's already paid."

"With what?"

She knew him too well.

"Like I said. It's paid. What's the Dwarf up to?"

Fox looked toward the stables. "Collecting his gold. It'll take him days. I was really looking forward to seeing him covered in stinking pollen."

She looked at the sky. It had begun to snow again. "We should head south."

"Maybe."

Jacob felt under his shirt for the imprint of the moth.

"You have maybe a year."

Well? A lot could be done in a year. In this world, there was a cure for everything.

He only had to find it. Somewhere.

Jacob thought
that saving his brother
would be the greatest
challenge he'd ever
have to face.

He was wrong.

DON'T MISS THE NEXT
RECKLESS
ADVENTURE

COMING SOON